D-39

A ROBODOG'S JOURNEY

Irene Latham

i◠i Charlesbridge

Published by Charlesbridge
9 Galen Street, Watertown, MA 02472
(617) 926-0329
www.charlesbridge.com

Library of Congress Cataloging-in-Publication Data
Names: Latham, Irene, author. | Green, Jamie, illustrator.
Title: D-39 : a robodog's journey / by Irene Latham ; illustrated by
    Jamie Green.
Other titles: D-thirty-nine
Description: Watertown, MA : Charlesbridge Publishing, undefined |
    Summary: "A robodog, D-39, and his human friends discover
    challenges, danger, and the strength to persevere in this war and
    survival dystopian novel in verse about friendship and family"—
    Provided by publisher.
Identifiers: LCCN 2020017273 (print) | LCCN 2020017274 (ebook) |
    ISBN 9781623541811 (hardcover) | ISBN 9781632899729 (ebook)
Subjects: CYAC: Novels in verse. | Dogs—Fiction. | Robots—Fiction. |
    Survival—Fiction. | War—Fiction. | Science fiction.
Classification: LCC PZ7.5.L39 Daal 2021 (print) | LCC PZ7.5.L39 (ebook) |
    DDC [Fic]—dc23
LC record available at https://lccn.loc.gov/2020017273
LC ebook record available at https://lccn.loc.gov/2020017274

Printed in the United States of America
(hc) 10 9 8 7 6 5 4 3 2 1

Illustrations done on iPad using Procreate software
Display type set in ITC Officina Sans Bold by Adobe Systems Inc.
Text type set in ITC Officina Serif Book by Adobe Systems Inc.
Printed by Berryville Graphics in Berryville, Virginia, USA
Production supervision by Jennifer Most Delaney
Designed by Cathleen Schaad

Especially for Eric—
son, friend, muse, hero.

I.

Hey Hi Ho There

It's me, Klynt Tovis, coming to you live from a looganut farm in the Worselands. I click the button on the ham, ears alert for a reply. I'm not supposed to talk to strangers, even on an old ham radio—especially now that even low-power unlicensed broadcasts are against the law. But now that I've unburied myself from the heap of wires and metal parts in my room, and now that I've finally gotten a signal, how can I not try it? Besides, does it really count if no one is around to listen?

Listen

If you are alive and haven't left for greener prairies, and if anyone is listening, here's the latest: It's another hotseason day of me feeling like I'm going to drown in the hum-nothing that is the Worselands. No sound for miles except flickering stream-screen static and the low rumble of Papa's chug-chug churning the dirt patchwork.

All morning I've been working on the ham, because that's what restoration experts do—maintain our collections. This ham now joins ranks with a rotary dial telephone—complete with cord—an old typewriter, and a printing press! Yes, each and every one actually works.

Hear that, Mama? You're not the only one making a difference in the world. Come home and I'll show you my Museum of Fond Memories. You won't be sorry, I promise.

Promise

Over and out, I say, and click off the ham.
It'd be so much more satisfying if someone
actually answered. But for now, all I can do
is keep hoping and tinkering.

And then, at the noon ticktock strike—
when Papa promised he would come in
from the fields, but of course he doesn't,
because nothing matters more than producing a lucrative crop of looganuts—I
hear a bzz-squeal-thump. And it isn't the
old cockadoodle weather vane chasing a
blusterblow. No. The air is completely still.
Bzzz-squeal-thump-THUMP. Not weather.
Not human. Unmistakably robo.

Robo

Robo, short for robot.

Not that robos are all that practical in the middle of a deathstretch. Things have been even worse since the old president died and his we-thought-he'd-be-better-but-he's-not son took over—the second President Vex. This isn't the time to think about itchglitchy robos that guzzle m-fuel. M-fuel is pretty much nonexistent these days, and no way will Papa let me keep a robo anyway.

But that's not the point.

The Point

A robo would make a fine addition to my collection—a pièce de résistance. Especially if it's an antique model. Above all, Mama would love it. Maybe even more than my newly operational printing press. She'd be button-popping impressed! Plus it's something to do other than what I'm supposed to be doing, which is sparkshining and stocking the burrow in case the deathstretch reaches the Worselands the way the streamscreen says it will.

I sure hope the streamscreen is wrong.

Wrong

No one should have to worry about taking shelter inside a burrow, where there's no sky, no privacy, no freedom. It doesn't make sense. But that's the world we live in.

Our burrow is nothing more than a hole in the ground. It's got a hatch that's hidden beneath the old plastic sandbox, and inside there are pegs for stairs and wooden shelves that I've been sparkshining and stocking for days.

Thank goodness it's less than a week before hotseason break is over and I'll go back to school. That's great, but also not great, because going to school means chores ram-jammed into just a few after-school hours and homework to boot. No knockaround time in my bedroom and the Museum of Fond Memories.

I keep myself very still as I listen again for what I think is a robo. I don't even breathe, because I'm listening so hard to determine where the sound is coming from. I hear a bzzzz, then the clatter of tools.

The barn. Of course!

Of Course

If there's a robo, no doubt it's thirsty and desperate. Its chestplate might already show the red rings of death. Which means I've got to hurry. It's a lot harder to revive a bzzflopped robo than it is to simply sparkshine one up.

I pat my pocket for my trusty screwdriver, which is as effective a weapon as it is a restoration tool—just in case it isn't a robo—and I spring for the door. I keep my footsteps red-fox light, of course, and make sure the screen door doesn't slap behind me so I don't spook the robo. They can be sensitive.

Or as Papa would say, robos are a pain in the you-know-what. Papa. Known to the rest of the world as Link Tovis.

Link Tovis

Once the owner, now Papa is merely the operator of Anchor T Farm, since President Vex ordered government officials to seize everyone's land. We pay rent to live here.

Thank goodness Papa's out dusting the far west field. I spot his rusty chug-chug, looking like a tiny boat riding an endless green waterworld. The stalks crinkle and rustle as if they're saying hello.

I know what Papa would do with a robo. I shuddershake as an image comes into my head of Papa armed with his slingblade. Or worse, swinging a hammer. Scrap metal is still worth something because it can be reshaped, melted, molded. And some robo parts might prove useful.

But I am a curator, a restoration expert. Until I've had a good look, no way will I allow that kind of destruction. Not when a robodog might be the very thing to bring Mama home to the Anchor T.

The Anchor T

The Anchor T farmhouse sits like an island, abandoned in the middle of a looganut sea. The only other house for miles belongs to the Tannins, and it's nearly a mile away. Sometimes it feels like Papa and I are the only people in the whole bigsky world.

But not today.

Today

I jog across the dirtdusty yard, listening for the robo. The barn door squeals like a prairie-falcon call as I push it with one finger so it will open slowly—oh so slowly. I watch the patch of light spread across the dirt floor. My eyes scan the toolboxes and soilnurture equipment.

Nothing.

My heart thudjams as I step inside and inhale deeply. The barn doesn't smell like hay or manure the way a livestock barn would. Better. It holds the scent of metal and machines and the faintest whiff of gasoline. Heaven for a restoration expert like me.

I lift my hands, and I make my movements so slow it feels like I'm suspended in a jelly-jar. *Hey hi ho there*, I sweetmurmur. *I come in peace.*

Whirr-click-click. *Arf, arf, arf!* Three alarming barks that even babies know mean the robo is requesting assistance.

Assistance

When my eyes finally find the robo, I suck in my breath. It's wearing a bandana. Only the top-brand-of-its-day Dog Alive robodogs have those. Can it be? Of all the robos in all the world, the kind with the most ambitious programming is what turns up in our barn?

I zero in on its chestplate. Yes. There it is, the Dog Alive logo. By some miracle I've got myself a dented, scratchpatched, how-can-it-possibly-be-functioning, first-gen D-39 robodog! *Wow.*

No red rings of death, thank goodness. But a flashing yellow light tells me this robo needs my help. Right away. I hold out my hand so it can sniff me, and it rewards me with a squeaky tailwag. *Hey hi ho there, fella.* I quirkface when it licks me. So real-looking, which is what Dog Alive was known for. And still operational. It could be an actual golden retriever, complete with the thirty-nine pairs of chromosomes that all dogs have, which is how this model got its name. Amazing. Mama would love it.

Well, she'd definitely love it more if it were a real dog. But here in the Worselands, that's impossible.

Impossible

I am not a robo expert. I'm better with simple machines, the older the better. Robos are too recent. But even a curator like me can appreciate newfangled tech modeled after something that's almost extinct, like a dog.

There aren't any real dogs left here or in our entire country, thanks to BrkX, a sickness so powerful scientists feared it would be impossible to stop. Which is why, I guess, old President Vex did what he did. Three years after I was born, he ordered Operation Eradication nation-wide when BrkX started to spread from dogs to humans and very nearly wiped out one entire city on the Gulf Coast. All dogs, healthy or not, were euthanized. All of them. Yes, it stopped the spread of the sickness to humans. But was it really necessary? People were flipfurious. So the government offered to replace dogs with robos—that was their solution.

And they were zapjawed when people started rioting. People dumped the robos, using them to barricade city streets in protest.

A robo to replace a real-live, well-loved dog. What a sick consolation prize.

Prize

It's not a flesh-and-blood dog, but a D-39 is something special. A top-grade acquisition. At least it is to me, someone who's never seen a real dog, except in books and on the streamscreen. And I know enough about robos to know what this one needs: a washdown, a charge, and a fill-up.

Which stinks, because pretty much no one has enough m-fuel these days, thanks to the government seizing control of the refineries. It's so valuable, Papa keeps our last cans stashed in a hideyhole in the burrow. The chug-chug won't run without m-fuel, and according to the streamscreen, people have killed for the stuff.

I stroke the robo's head. *It's okay.* Whirr-click-click. *Arf, arf, arrrrr* . . . The robo cocks its head, its dark eyes deepening to black, and when the chestplate starts buzzing, I know we're running out of time. If I don't do something, this is the end of the line.

End of the Line

Don't bzzflop on me, I tell it as I back out of the barn. As soon as I'm out of the way, sunlight illuminates the robo. It sits as still as a sphinx, except for its tail, which swishswipes gentle as freshwash.

The bandana tied around its neck is red—like the one Papa wears. That's when I decide it's a he. With robos you can choose whatever gender you want it to be.

My mind whipwhirls, then stops. M-fuel. The answer to this problem begins and ends with m-fuel. *I'll be back in a jingle-snap.* I pull the door closed and race for the burrow. I can't think about Papa right now. I can't think about his rules and every-thing he's taught me about preparation and preservation—about being smart so we can survive the deathstretch.

Even though the fighting hasn't gotten to us out here in the Worselands, we all know it could. It's more likely now than ever, with the new President Vex in charge.

He's even more ruthless than his father, if that's possible. I mean, the first Vex outlawed dogs!

I've got to get some m-fuel. Just a little bit. Enough to keep the D-39 operational.

Operational

After I've poured the m-fuel into the little opening on D-39's chestplate, I can't believe how light I feel. The m-fuel can feels pretty light, too. I swallow. Papa is going to go jayballs.

I shake my head. I'll deal with it later. For now, all I can do is stare at the now fully operational robo. A D-39! Here at the Anchor T! It's the best thing that's happened all hotseason. Something new-old to tinker with. Something that just might actually bring Mama home.

I quirkface. This definitely beats all the time I've spent reading Mama's old vet-school textbooks, fingering her name in each one—*Ersu Tovis*. The books with her actual handwriting and highlighted text passages that give me a peek inside her head. What a gift.

Gift

And now a D-39. Like it's my birthday, or some other holiday that includes wrapping paper and shiny ribbon.

I can teach him tricks, and he can sleep with me, and keep me company while Papa is busy doing whatever it is he does all day out in the fields.

D-39 is one of the most realistic-looking models. It came out before retailers figured out that slick metal is easier to keep up than faux fur. And a robo that eats and poops is a lot more trouble than one without normal body functions. The D-39 has a small solar panel on the top of its head, which requires owners to get outside with their robos—when most folks would rather be inside plugged into their devices or watching the streamscreen.

And those weren't the only complaints.

Complaints

At first all the D-39 does is bark. *Arf, arf, arf, arf, arf!*

When I hear the chug-chug getting closer to the house, I hurry the D-39 to the burrow. *You've just got to stay down here. For a little while. Give me a chance to boil Papa like a frog.* I plan to start the conversation easy, as if I want to get a robodog, before I tell him I actually already have one. If I'm not careful, Papa's likely to reject the idea of a robo right away. It's one of my biggest complaints about my father—how stubborn he is. Once his mind is set, there's pretty much no budging him.

The robo licks my hand, and his tail jerk-wags. I can't help it: I quirkface. I haven't been this joyslammed in eons. *Arf, arf, arf, arf!* The D-39 is joyslammed, too. *Shhh,* I remind him, and I monkey-climb up the pegs. I can still hear my new robo as I close the hatch. I just pray Papa can't.

Can't

Did I mention it's quiet in the Worselands? The hum-nothing stretches for miles. Which is why as soon as Papa cuts the engine on the chug-chug, I can hear it, even from far across the yard at the edge of the field. *Arf, arf, arf, arf, arf, arf!*

I cough and hurryscurry toward Papa. *How's the crop, Papa? Everything good with the looganuts?* I whiprattle on, praying Papa can't hear the barking, at least not yet. Not before I figure out a way to persuade him we should keep the robo. But my papa—he's too smart.

Too Smart

Papa scowls and puts his hand up. *Hear that, Klynt?* He strides toward the burrow right away. *Sounds like a lost gobbler.* I hurryscurry to keep up. *It's not a gobbler.* He stops. I can almost see the neurons in his brain pulsing. *Something you need to tell me, Klynt?* I take a breath, not sure how I should spin this. Papa's not the only too-smart one around here. Do I tell him how joyslammed I am, or do I downplay it? I take in his droopbottom face and the awkward position of his shoulders. He's tired, and probably aching again. Best to stick to revealing less rather than more. *It's just an old robo,* I say. *I thought it might prove useful.*

Useful

Papa's face lightens slightly. *A robo? Here?* I nod. *Yes. A D-39.*

D-39. That's the model with the fur, right? The solar/m-fuel hybrid? When I nod again, he squinches his lips. *Hmmm. And you put it in the burrow?*

I know right away what Papa is thinking. He's got a calculator in his head. *Yes, sir. He's a little scratchpatched, but completely operational. Maybe useful.* I figure mentioning that again can't hurt.

Papa's cheeks lift, and he almost quirkfaces. Almost. *Good job, sugar girl. Now that all the robotech has moved away from m-fuel, a D-39's got to be rare. Could bring in good currency. Even a deathstretch can't kill off the collectibles trade. And if that doesn't pan out, it's possible the robo at least has some valuable parts. Why don't you sparkshine it and then bring it up to the house? And please put some tape over its speakers! Can't think with all that racket. We'll see what we've got.*

What We've Got

As I lead the D-39 across the yard, I sweet-murmur. *Never mind him. I think you're worth something just as you are. Even if it doesn't fatten our pockets. Even if you are dirty and loud and outdated.* The words are really more for me.

I wish I knew how to make the robo do things, to make him valuable to us, to the Anchor T. As a whole, not only for his parts. But he hasn't exactly come packing a manual. Which means it will take lots of trial and error. And it's not like I have a ton of robo experience. Or real-life animal experience, either.

All I know I've learned from Mama's vet books. *Please stop barking,* I say as I take off the bandana to sponge him down and tease the tangles from his fur. He cocks his head, as if he's considering whether I'm worthy enough to be his pack leader, or whether he should obey me.

He barks some more, and even with the tape over his speakers, it's still loud. He's got a speaker embedded in his throat, apparently. No way I can tape that without hardwiping him and taking him apart.

Finally I'm done, and Papa gives the robo a quick once-over. *Hmmm. Looks good. Real good. Could fetch a nice price as is at the pit.*

The Pit

I swallow, and my stomach turns slip-sloppy. He's talking about the salvage pit. It's almost as bad as if Papa had swung the hammer. The result would be the same: no more robo. And my chance to get Mama back to the Anchor T would be gone.

Papa, please let's keep him, just for a little while? I promise he won't be any trouble.

Trouble

Papa sighs. *You know we can't do that, sugar girl. We need ammo. Food. And the robo requires m-fuel.* My heart fistclenches. I don't dare tell him about the m-fuel I already used.

We should make a trip to the pit before school starts, Papa adds. *While the roads are still empty.* Classes starting again will mean families who have stayed on their farm all hotseason will venture forth—which means the drifters squatting on abandoned farms will come out, too. That'll make the roads less safe.

Papa's eyes glimmerspark. *Can't wait to see what Gloria will give us.* I grab Papa's hand. I have to think of something to convince him that me having a robo won't be any trouble. *Please, Papa,* I start. Then it comes to me. The one thing with any sort of power to possibly turn Papa's mind. I yank my hand away from his. *Mama would let me keep him.*

Silence hangs as heavy as river fogsteam between us. So heavy that I don't dare breathe. And that's when the D-39 saves me: *arf, arf, arf, arf!* The fogsteam lifts as my robo starts barking again.

Again

Papa's face turns humpgrump and his voice jagged as lightning. *You need to reset it*, he says. But I don't want to hardwipe D-39. I can't. There's something in his deepdark gaze that makes me think he knows things that I don't want erased.

Like the way the world used to be before BrkX, when real dogs snoozed on front porches and Mama was still here. In some odd way D-39 feels like a link to that time. Who knows what adventures he's had? He barks again.

Hush, D-39, I try. Because if I can't get him quiet, there's not a chance Papa will let me keep him. When D-39 doesn't respond, I move on to other words. *No. Quiet. Stop.* He still barks until Papa lifts up from his seat. *Enough!*

Enough

D-39 whimpers and wets the floor. *Why does it have to be one of* those *models?* Papa says. *No wonder someone dumped him.*

Papa is not a fan of messes. Or of anything that requires his attention when he'd rather be doing something else.

The screen door slaps behind him as Papa heads out to the porch, and I'm glad he's gone. I tidywipe the wet spot and write in my notebook: *Enough=stop.*

I pull D-39 into my lap, all flutterbugged and scratchpatched. When he looks up at me, his eyes say that in all the world, I'm his favorite. *Me.* A girl who's nobody's favorite. I save up the feeling to enjoy again later.

Later

When Papa comes in to cozy in his chair, he doesn't even say hey hi ho there. But his mouth is soft, and he carefully steps over the sleeping D-39, which means he's not flipfurious anymore.

As soon as he sits down, he clicks on the streamscreen to listen to the latest reports about gun-marches and boomblasts that rock all the big cities. *See?* he says. *It's a good thing we live in the Worselands.*

I shrug. It's an old argument between us. He loves the Worselands, and I don't. But tonight he's right.

Right

There are advantages to quiet and loneliness. We don't get marches and boomblasts here. And sometimes people even dump treasures like D-39.

But then a special report: *Today a rash of superboomblasts spread coast to coast, all in public buildings.*

It's the Patriots, protesting the latest decrees passed by the government, which no longer works for the people, not really. These days it works only for the president and his crooked cronies. Whatever President Vex wants, President Vex gets—even if it's not right—and all those politicians get rewarded with currency and property and power. Meanwhile the rest of us suffer shortages and violence.

Freedom! Freedom! Freedom! the Patriots shout on the streamscreen. President Vex makes an announcement: *For safety, no more school.*

School

I've got to talk to someone, so I fire up the ham. *Hey hi ho there, can you believe it? The government sent soldiers to board up and padlock the schools, even here in the Worselands, which everyone knows is the least populated place in the country.*

We won't go back to school this leafseason. Instead we get an extra-long hotseason. Is anyone out there listening?

Apparently not, because I check every channel and still get no response.

That evening the kids they show on the streamscreen quirkface and high-five, like no school is the best thing ever.

Not for me. Because once D-39 is gone, no more school will mean that all day every day, it'll just be me and Papa again. A recipe for disaster.

Disaster

The next day a late hotseason blusterblow sweeps across all of the looganut fields, shriveling a bunch of blossoms.

The good news is we don't have time to go to the pit. But right away Papa's temper flares, glows hot as the pipe he smokes every night. *This is the last thing we need right now,* he grumbles as he pulls me into the fields with him. Even with two of us working nonstop, it will still take several days to do damage control. Any plants with shrivels must be removed immediately.

Papa barely gives me a chance to pull on my gloves and get a sip of water, much less fussfidget with D-39, who might be useful if I could figure out his programming. *Faster, Klynt! We've got to beat this thing. Otherwise we might lose the whole crop.*

The Whole Crop

I'm trying, I say. My hand and fingers ache from curling around my blade. I'm always trying, but I'm no good at soilnurture. Not like Papa.

The only thing that makes it bearable is the way D-39 stays nearby almost all day— sometimes in sleepmode, sometimes nosing around in the dirt. My favorite thing is when he bumps his head against my leg, letting me know he's with me.

I can appreciate Papa's old-school farming methods in theory. I really can. I just don't like actually performing the tasks. Mostly I hate the dirt and the sun and the digging—*especially* the digging.

I think D-39 senses how I feel, because when I'm digging he lopes over and snags my right work glove with his teeth. My cheeks lift. He's so tender about it, and he's so proud of his catch once it's dangling from his mouth, it's hard to be stern with him the way I know I must. If his program is ever going to learn what he's supposed to do and what he shouldn't, I have to teach him.

When I pat D-39's head and command, *Leave it*, he does. As he wanders off, I'm grateful that his red bandana makes him easy to spot—like Papa.

It doesn't change the fact that I'd rather do just about anything—even must-dos like dishes and mopping and sparkshining the poopflush—than work the looganuts.

Stupid looganuts. Stupid farm. Acres and acres of hum-nothing.

Hum-Nothing

A week passes before Papa mentions the pit again. *Klynt, let's talk about the D-39.* His eyes glimmerspark, and he's nearly quirkfacing, so I know he's up to some sort of mischief. That means he must be joyslammed about how things are going in the field.

Care to strike a bargain? he asks. I meet his eyes, and he continues. *Harvesttime will be here soon. And with no one left in the Worselands to help bring in the crop, I need you, Klynt.*

I open my mouth to say something teasing like *I thought you loved the hum-nothing of the Worselands.* But he lifts his hand to stop me from saying anything yet. So I hard-press my lips and wait. *Now I know you'd rather be in school, but you're not. And with both of us working, it will go twice as fast.*

Wow, Papa. This time I can't stop myself. *I don't even need school with you here to teach me math.*

He quirkfaces for real and nudges my shoulder. *Okay, sugar girl. Here's the deal: as long as you help in the fields—without complaining—you can keep the D-39.*

Keep the D-39

No way can I hide the joyslam that rushes through me. I leap up and grab Papa in a quick upcuddle. And then I throw my arms around D-39 and let him lick my face.

It's an amazing deal. I'd have to help Papa in the fields anyway, because we're a team. Even though I had been hoping to work on restoring a VCR so we might watch some old movies. *But what if school starts back? And I* can't *help with the harvest. Can I still keep D-39?*

He takes a breath. *I don't think school's going to reopen anytime soon.* His face is grim. *A government without the consent of its people cannot stand. Things will get worse before they get better, sugar girl.*

D-39 bumps his head against my thigh. There's only one answer. I hold out my hand to Papa. *You've got yourself a deal.* His quirk is so bigsky it takes up his whole face. Then it fades. *I'm sorry we have to make deals like this, sugar girl.*

I know he's talking about President Vex and the deathstretch. *Is the fighting ever going to end, Papa? Will the robosoldiers and boomblasts find us here on the Anchor T?*

His face folds into a frown, and I want to take my question back. *I wish I knew, sugar girl.* He pats my leg, then D-39's head. *Nothing lasts forever, does it? To everything there is a season.*

A Season

Papa is right. School doesn't start again, and somehow we bring the harvest in—just me and Papa and D-39. The days fold into one another, easyeasy. While Papa takes stock and makes preparations for the next crop of looganuts, I tinker in my museum, with D-39 on the floor beside me.

It's as if the ticktock has stopped, and we are stuck in the eye of a hurricane that has no name. All is calm.

And then it happens—the season shifts. *Turn in your weapons*, President Vex orders on the streamscreen. He's talking about guns. *We have nothing left*, the Patriots retort. *You can't take our guns, too!*

Violence erupts as officers go door to door, trying to collect. Some people take a stand and refuse to hand over their guns. The death toll rises on both sides. What will it be like—how will we survive—when one side has all the weapons?

Weapons

Papa polishes his gun until it gleams. He got it from his father, who got it from his father. No way will he voluntarily turn it in. *They'll have to ripclaw it from my hands*, he says. As he inventories ammunition, he grumbles. *First our pets and livestock, then our land. Now our guns. When will it end?*

His eyes turn hard and shiny like ripe looganuts as he hands me an old slingshot to go with my screwdriver—two weapons no one's trying to take yet. *We can't give up, Klynt. We can't give in now.* I nod and keep a hand on D-39's shoulder blade. Such a simple thing, but it steadies me.

I wish I could understand it all, what's happening in our country. It's so complicated, and part of me doesn't even want to try. I'd rather fix the sticky question-mark key on my old typewriter, even though I know it'll only last a few keystrokes before it's sticky again.

Papa curses when the streamscreen dubs the deathstretch "the *New* Civil Crisis." As if to minimize what's really happening.

I think we're beyond calling it a crisis. He shakes his head. *Nothing new about it, just more of the government taking away our rights, ignoring our God-given freedoms.*

I don't say anything, because my words won't help. Next time I get on the ham, though, I think I'll pose this question, and maybe someone will answer: How can the deathstretch be "new" when terrible things have been happening since way back when I was a baby?

When I Was a Baby

Mama lived with us here, in the Worselands. While Papa tended the looganuts, she ran a vet clinic for large animals—horses and cows mostly.

Then BrkX swept across the country, and Mama was forced to be part of the Eradication. The government sent her a letter. *Dear Dr. Ersu Tovis*. It said vets had to be the ones to sink the needle in and also dispose of the dog bodies.

Papa says Mama wouldn't do it, couldn't do it. And that's when she and some others started the K-9 Corridor.

The K-9 Corridor

Modeled after the Underground Railroad during an earlier deathstretch, except this time it's for dogs. A secret network of people committed to saving dogs by moving them out of the Worselands or wherever else, and into the Wilds.

The Wilds, which is in another country with a different government and different rules. Where they quarantine dogs instead of killing them. Where they are experimenting with alternative treatments and working on a BrkX vaccine.

Everything to do with the K-9 Corridor is top secret. Punishable by death. It marked the beginning of Mama's life as an outlaw hero—and it also marked an end.

An End

Someone had to be in charge of taking care of the dogs once they made it to the end of their journey to the Wilds, and Mama decided it should be her. That's what a hero does, apparently—leaves.

It didn't help when the first President Vex raised taxes so high, no one could afford to keep their land. The law became "pay up or move out."

Mama set up a vet practice in the Wilds to save the dogs, yes, but also to try and help pay back taxes in order to keep Anchor T Farm. So our family wouldn't have to leave. Because Papa. The looganuts. The Worselands. It's our home.

Mama couldn't have known that a few years later the government would pass a law with jayballs interest rates and even more jayballs time limits for paying back debts. Whatever currency she sent home would never be enough. And then the heist of the century: President Vex took over the deed to the Anchor T and thousands of other farms across the country. Now we're like sharecroppers—for the government.

And still, for as long as there was mail delivery, Mama sent currency home to us. Did I mention that she's a hero?

Hero

Mama was supposed to be gone only one hotseason, but one hotseason turned into nine years.

If it weren't for this one photograph, I wouldn't remember her at all. To think she's only forty miles away! But with the death-stretch, the closed borders, the untamed land, the dogs and all their needs—she may as well be across ten thousand waterworlds.

I can't help it. I gravitate toward the ham. *Hey hi ho there. Anyone out there listening— Mama, if YOU are listening—you should come back now. We have D-39, who's not a real dog, I know, but at least he's something. You've been a hero long enough.*

The three of us are here. I swallow and click off the ham. I sweetmurmur into D-39's scratchpatched ear, *We're waiting.*

Waiting

More superboomblasts. More death. Roads too treacherous to risk driving anywhere.

Papa keeps to himself, making repairs in the burrow or in the barn. I upcuddle D-39 and read the canine sections in Mama's vet books to him. It settles him right into sleepmode.

My mind fills with thoughts of Mama.

Mama

Sometimes I hear her voice. She says things like, *Listen to your father*, or once when I was on the creekbank alone, *Turn around*.

I did turn around, and there, in the place where I was about to sit, was a giant zapper nest. If Mama hadn't spoken, the bottom half of my body would have no doubt been embellished with stinging welts.

When I told Papa about it, he shook his head. *That's not your mama, Klynt.* He grabbed me by the shoulders, shook me hard. *Do you hear me, Klynt? Your mama's dead. She's never coming back.*

But I don't believe him. No. Mama went to the Wilds so she could save all those dogs. So she could work as a vet. And that's exactly what she's doing.

Mama's coming back. Just as soon as things settle down. As soon as it's safe here in the Worselands. And as soon as the K-9 Corridor can operate without her. She's probably training new K-9 Corridor volunteers right now. A new vet to take her place. The work must go on. I get that.

Those other words are just Papa's way of keeping us from missing her too much. Not the truth.

The Truth

I've never believed it whenever Papa says Mama is dead—that she died in border crossfire. How can I, when I hear her sweetmurmur so loud, so clear?

It's like when it comes to people. Papa only believes what he sees, which is jay-balls, because he has all kinds of faith in looganuts and how they grow from nearly invisible seeds into blooms that produce more seeds that can be ground into meal or from which oil can be extracted.

Papa's skepticism is why I've never told him the truth. That Mama says to me almost every day now: *Come to Everlake. You'll be safe at Everlake where everyone is free.*

Where Everyone Is Free

Hey hi ho there. I lean in close to the ham.
*If you're listening, Mama, could you send me
a signal? The telegraph, the printing press,
the ham—they're all me trying to reach you.*
D-39 settles at my feet, so I rub his belly
with my toes. *Please tell me more about
Everlake.*

I click off the ham. I'm not sure how to
tell Mama that I want more than the basic
facts. Because I already know Everlake is
across the border in the Wilds, only forty
miles away from the Anchor T. I know there
are no paved roads across those forty miles
of forest—only hunting trails and acres of
hum-nothing.

I also know Everlake started as an artists'
colony, and getting there is like finding a
pot of gold at the end of a rainbow. Only
instead of sliding down a beam of light,
you have to locate and hike a remote trail
marked by leafgiants paintslashed with
the color blue. Papa says that if you keep
walking, eventually you find the original
K-9 Corridor shelter full of real dogs.

What I want to know is what it's like to live there with Mama and those real dogs, beside neighbors who are brushpainters and needlebenders. Who knows what treasures I might find there for my Museum of Fond Memories? Who knows what kind of life we might have together in the Wilds, where there is no deathstretch and everyone is free? Right now, here in the Worselands, freedom feels like a fantasy.

Fantasy

It doesn't help that all my friends and all our neighbors—except the Tannins—have recently headed out. Escaped to the Wilds following the promise of a better life any-place else.

Since the schools closed, we've even lost the families I thought would never leave. Because no deathstretch in the Wilds means no boomblasts, no shortages, no government taking personal property. No fear of starvation and death. Those things are happening here, in our country.

Up in the Wilds, schools are still open. Freezeseasons may last half the year, but when hotseason comes, no one tells you what you can or can't plant and grow. Freedom isn't just a dream. And maybe best of all, if you're part of the K-9 Corridor, in the Wilds there are dogs aplenty.

Aplenty

Papa says the farmers who left will all be sorry when the deathstretch ends and their looganut farms are in shambles while ours is growing plentiful and green as anything.

When the streamscreen reports something about the rising population of dogs in the Wilds in spite of another failed vaccine for BrkX, I jump up, move closer so I don't miss a word. It's a relief to hear good news for a change, even if it's not happening in the Worselands. It's close enough to fill me with hope.

But then the sound turns crackly, and we can't hear any words at all. *Did you hear that?* I say to Papa. *More dogs! Real ones!* D-39 swishswipes his tail like this news makes him happy, too.

Papa nods, and when his voice comes, it's thick. *Wouldn't have been possible without your mama.* I know he's proud of Mama, just like I am.

I suck in my breath. I know I'm pushing it, but I can't help it. I have to know more about Mama. *How could you let her go?* I ask. He sucks on his pipe, stares at the fuzz on the streamscreen. *I couldn't have stopped her, sugar girl. Even if I tried. As soon as she got the idea to start the K-9 Corridor, she might have been with us in body, but her spirit was already gone to the Wilds. I helped as much as I could, even when it was just listening to all her plans and setbacks. She wasn't one to stand by, even before the K-9 Corridor. She liked to keep busy.*

I get that. I, too, like to be busy.

Busy

I sink my fingers into D-39's faux fur and wonder what real dog fur feels like. Is it silkier than this?

I want to ask Papa if Mama's voice has ever come to him the way it keeps coming to me, but I don't want to shut down the conversation. Any words about Mama are good words, and if I'm quiet, a few more might slip out of his mouth before he catches himself.

We're lucky here in the Worselands, he says. *The Anchor T is a classroom. Here you can study whatever you want. Plus, there's plenty to keep us busy for years.*

I sigh. With those words we're right back to my no-Mama life. And I know what Papa really means about being able to study what I want. More like, here at the Anchor T, I can study what *he* wants.

What He Wants

We focus on soilnurture basics—plant, hoe, weed. When I can't stand it anymore, Papa lets me go in early to wash up and tinker with the VCR. There's only so much I can repair without a welder or new parts, but I do what I can.

But then one side—Patriots or President Vex, who knows which—shuts down the satellites. In the time it takes to strike a match, no more static. No more streamscreen.

I can't help it. I throw a book against the wall and glare at Papa. D-39 whines and positions himself right on top of my feet, in protector mode. He wants to keep us both safe. *We should have left when everyone else did*, I say. *We should have crossed the border.*

The Border

Way back in kinderschool, I learned there are eighteen crossings on the Worselands–Wilds border. All of them are closed now, thanks to President Vex. The walls once intended to keep others out of our country are now used to keep us in. The only way to cross is illegally. If you make it—and many don't—then you might get stuck in a refugee camp for months or even years.

The fighting may not be in the Worselands yet, but with each passing week of the leafseason things feel tighter, more tense. Like we're trapped.

Even Papa can't maintain his optimism about our decision to keep the farm going instead of giving it up for the uncertainty of refugee status. He no longer whistles while he works the looganuts. His brow stays creased all the time, and I do my best to stay out of the way.

I spend my time teaching D-39 how to shake and beg and stay. The command *come* is the toughest. Sometimes he pretends not to listen to me. But I know if I am patient and consistent, his programming will catch on.

From time to time in the evenings when Papa and I are in the same room, one of us clicks the button on the streamscreen remote control, just to check. But whatever the hour, all we get now is fuzz.

Fuzz

Most nights we take our plates out to the porch, watch the Worselands sky stretch and yawn over the flats and humpbacks as we eat our canned meatscramble—which isn't meat at all.

The humpbacks really do look like fuzzy whales breeching in a black waterworld on these late-leafseason evenings. Papa lights his pipe and clicks on the emergency broadcaster so we can listen to the single station that every once in a while rides an outlaw airwave to our ears.

D-39 listens, too. His ears perk and cock, as if he's trying to understand the odd sounds. Between unofficial reports . . . *food shortages zonewide . . . today thousands dead . . . deadliest day of fighting since the New Civil Crisis began* . . . and recorded boomblasts and ear-blistering static, we somehow gluestick together the latest news. Due to an uprising, President Vex has been evacuated to a safe house and more troops have been brought in to "keep the peace."

I clap my hand over my mouth, and I can't help it: my mind goes instantly to Mama. I hardpress my face into D-39's neck fur. Mama, if you're out there, if you can hear my voice the way I hear yours: Please tell me, how is this *peace*?

II.

Peace

The food shortages we've heard about on the emergency broadcaster finally reach the Worselands. Blockades prevent supply trucks from moving in or out, so we chomp looganuts for every meal. D-39 rests under the table while we eat, his eyes begging for treats.

The toaster that took me three months to fix sits idle. No wheatkins. And we're the lucky ones. At least we have looganuts, and there are no boomblasts outside our door.

President Vex and the Patriots agree that the first day of every month will be a cease-fire—one day of peace—so regular folks like us can stand in line to get wheatkins, redroots, beans. Only the basics and just enough to keep us alive.

We all downcount to rations day.

Rations Day

Papa and I walk together to the Tannin family's house, so we can save oil and m-fuel by riding together in Dr. Tannin's van. My fingers stay tucked around D-39's collar because I don't know yet how he'll handle being around other people.

I'm still zapjawed that Papa let me bring D-39. He didn't say yes until I promised that I won't engage with strangers, and my robo will be on his best behavior.

So far, so good. D-39's done nothing but whine a little and prancedance. But the true test is how he handles a crowd.

Crowd

I quirkface when I see Jopa, who's only six, waiting for us outside the Tannin family's front door. *Hey hi ho there*, I call, and I command D-39 to stay when Jopa barrels over. *K-K!* Jopa says, and I open my arms to him, even though his nickname for me is a little silly.

He shoves his ever-present ant jar against my chest before he throws his arms around D-39, whose tail swishswipes. I hold the jar up to watch the harvester ants crowd the opening of the sand tunnel. *Looking good*, I say, even though I'm not a fan of ants the way Jopa is.

He quirkfaces between D-39's licks to his face. *Did you know each ant nest carries its own scent?* I waggle my eyebrows. *Really?* Jopa knows more about ants than anyone I've met. *He's so shiny*, Jopa says, arms still around D-39. *Except for the scratchpatched ear*, I say. I, too, love how shiny D-39 is and how the red bandana around his neck makes him look so dapper.

I tell Jopa about the barking, and how we finally got D-39 to quiet down by feeding him raw looganuts. And how D-39 will sit still for hours if he thinks it means he'll get a looganut treat. Jopa giggles. *I bet his programmer never thought of that.* Papa shakes his head. *Programmers in those days weren't thinking about utility, only entertainment. What a waste.*

D-39 is so much more than entertainment. He's my friend. He stays by my side. He licks my fingers. He listens. I understand more now about why Mama loves dogs so much. D-39's only a robo, but I love him. I really do. But I don't say it out loud. That kind of information feels far too tender for sharing.

Sharing

As they come out the door, we greet Jopa's grown-up sister, Tiev, and Dr. Tannin—whose first name Papa told me is Penny. But no one ever calls her that, because she is far too slick and shiny to be called the same name as some ancient copper coin.

It's weird seeing Dr. Tannin at home—she's usually at the clinic where she says it feels like she's the only doctor left in the Worselands. She treats everyday concerns like asthma and diabetes along with urgent-care things like broken bones.

Tiev's ponytail bobs as she does some quick squats and stretches—she wants to keep fit so she'll be ready for her track team as soon as the colleges open back up. *Just three quick sets*, she says. *Then we can go.*

As Tiev starts her second set of reps, I introduce Dr. Tannin to my robo. *Dog Alive, wow. That's a dinosaur.* Dr. Tannin even examines D-39's chestplate. *Looks like an early hybrid. No trouble with the solar panel?* Papa looks to me. *We're outdoors all the time,* I say quickly. Which is true and not true.

It seems like D-39's solar reserves have never worked properly, because the panels are cracked, and moisture has invaded the solar cells. Which means the small m-fuel engine inside his metal casing kicks in a lot. It sounds like a hummingbird as the m-fuel burns off and emits its clean, odorless gas through the narrow vents.

But I'm not ready yet to tell Papa about the m-fuel I'm still using to keep D-39 operational. Every drop matters. So I change the subject instead. *The only thing he came with was the bandana.* D-39 sits in his oh-so-still sphinx pose as I adjust the bright piece of fabric. *He appeared one day in the barn. Like magic.*

Magic

I block out Papa's voice as he tells Dr.
Tannin about the once-planned trip to the
pit. *You might do quite well on the parts*, Dr.
Tannin says. *No*, I say, making my voice
magically firm like hers—a voice that
people respect. *Papa and I made a deal.* As
Papa explains about our deal, I push my
shoulders back and buckle my seatbelt.
D-39 sits like a gentleman on the floor-
board in front of me like he's been riding
in vans forever. My robo relaxes so much
that he lolls out his black polka-dotted
tongue. *Looks like he's been eating ants*,
Jopa says. Dr. Tannin quirkfaces, meets
my eyes through the rearview mirror. *Nice
touch, the Chow tongue. Didn't know this
model had so many variations.*

Variations

We pass craggy buttes and vast tallgrass prairies lined with cold-dust fences. Every now and then there's a stand of leafgiants, but it's mostly unbroken sky. When we get to the school, we are given tickets—one per family. I can't believe the number of people in line. These are not my neighbors and classmates. Most are strangers. *Drifters, desperadoes*, Papa says. *Stay close.*

The line moves as slowly as the river during a drought, and I'm proud because D-39 obeys my every command. Who needs a manual? Not once does he jump or bark.

I like him, Jopa says. *He likes you*, I tell him. It's true. D-39 seems completely comfortable with his newest friend. I wonder, not for the first time, what my robo's life was like before he landed at the Anchor T. What commands did he learn and from whom?

As morning turns to afternoon, it's like we're inside a dream—not the nightmare we've heard about on the streamscreen. Everyone is friendly, kind. I overhear variations on conversations while we wait, and

I enjoy the way Papa's eyes brighten as he listens, argues, asks questions. For the first time in a long time, his humpgrump face is gone, at least for a few hours. He must get as humdrummed of me as I get of him.

I let out a big breath I didn't even know I was holding and catch the latest threads of Papa and Dr. Tannin's conversation. *Strange, isn't it?* Papa says. *This world we live in.* Dr. Tannin nods. *Getting more strange by the day.* I stroke D-39's scratch-patched ear as the conversation turns back to weather and news.

News

Superboomblasts last week in the south of the Worselands, Dr. Tannin says. *There is fighting headed our way.* Jopa's eyes bigsky as his mother describes that she's heard about flying robofighters coming out of nowhere. My eyes bigsky, too.

Papa clamps his jaw. *The fighting won't come to the northernmost Worselands. There's nothing here but farms.* Dr. Tannin puts her hands on her hips. *You're wrong, Link. There have been so many threats on Vex's life that he and his cabinet are running the country from a secret location. Things are about to come to a head. No one will be able to escape the violence, not even us.*

I hear Mama's voice: *she's right*. Mama— not just a hero for dogs. A hero for me. Sometimes my guide, sometimes my echo.

Echo

Jopa pulls back his lips to show me his new gap-toothed quirkface. *Tooth fairy brought me a chocolate nub!*

Chocolate. Chocolate. Chocolate. The word echoes in my mind, making my mouth as slipsloppy as D-39's. I haven't had chocolate in months.

Jopa lifts his ant jar. *I fed some to my ants. They like chocolate.* Dr. Tannin grabs Jopa's arm. *Shh, Jopa. You trying to start a riot?*

Riot

Sorry. Jopa shrugs but doesn't shrink. I wonder if it's living with a mom as forceful as Dr. Tannin that's made him strong.

Dr. Tannin leans in close to Papa. *Link, I've got the supplies we discussed.* Papa hard-presses an envelope into her hands before accepting the sack. Jopa rolls his eyes. *Mother wants us to sleep through the death-stretch.* Tiev glares, and Dr. Tannin's voice turns icy. *That's enough.* Jopa spins away from his mother in a riotous motion. *But it's true.*

That's not the point, Dr. Tannin growls, and I take a step back and grip D-39's neckfur. Because Jopa and I have this in common: Parents who like to tell us what the point is. As if we can't think for ourselves.

For Ourselves

That night Papa and I sit on the porch to eat our redroots and beans. As soon as we're done, Papa lights his pipe, and I watch the smoke whispertwitch into the cooling air. *How can a person sleep through a deathstretch?* I ask.

Papa keeps his gaze on the distant humpbacks. *Medication.* Papa sucks on the pipe. *If food runs out—if the looganuts stop producing, or if the government puts more restrictions in place—it's one way to save our own lives.* He faces me. *But I don't want you to worry about that. The farm is fine for now, and we've almost got the burrow stocked. You and I will stay right here on the Anchor T, where we belong. We have enough for ourselves.*

I shake my head. Sometimes I don't think he understands me at all. How can he talk to me about taking such drastic measures to stay in the Worselands when he knows how much I want to be with Mama? *This isn't where I belong.* The words are out of my mouth before I realize it.

Papa's eyes narrow into angerslits. *Careful, sugar girl. You think you know everything, but you don't.* I look away. I don't want to fight with him tonight. Not about Mama. I don't want to make bad memories.

Memories

My memories about Mama aren't really memories. Everything I know I learned from Papa. How she was born across the border at Everlake, and that's where she nursed an orphaned moose calf back to health and first knew she wanted to be a vet.

How Papa first met Mama when his best mare started favoring her right front foot. Mama came out to the Anchor T in her Dr. Ersu Tovis lab coat three days in a row. By the third day the mare was better, and my parents knew they wanted to be together forever.

Forever

A few months later, Mama moved to the farm. Three years after that, I was born. As the night air thickens, Papa extinguishes his pipe. I know the rest of the story: Forever turned out to be shorter than expected because of BrkX. Because Mama is a hero. Because Papa couldn't bear to leave the Anchor T, and Mama was always going to come back.

So many times I watched Papa ripclaw open envelopes from Mama. The currency was always wrapped in plain paper. No words anywhere for Papa or for me. That's how busy Mama is with her important work. She doesn't have time for anything but the essentials.

And then the envelopes stopped arriving. Months passed, years, and nothing. Now I'm twelve, and I know Mama only from a photograph. But the story's not over. There's more.

More

I can't think about what Papa says happened next. I can't think of what Papa says happened to Mama at the border, because it *didn't* happen. It couldn't have.

I squintcheck my eyes at Papa. It's his fault Mama left—him and his farm and his precious looganuts. I retreat to my museum. I think about getting on the ham, but I'm too tired. And what more would I say?

Instead, I sit with D-39. I tell him my secret thoughts, and his brown eyes glow, like he's really listening. *It's Papa's fault*, I say. It's because of him we're a family of two.

Two

The next morning Papa grinds looganuts into butter and smears the paste across a wheatkin for breakfast, but he doesn't dash to the looganut fields. *Follow me,* he says. We hike past the old swing set where I still play sometimes with Jopa, to the plastic sandbox that does nothing now except collect freshwash. Papa pushes it aside to reveal the round metal hatch.

The hatch creaks as he pulls it open, and when he shines his light inside, I see two cots shoved up against the wooden shelves that span the dirt-walled room. *Wow,* I say. Two blankets and two pillows. He places a hand on my shoulder. *Might need to be sleeping down here soon. Now we're ready, just in case.*

Just in Case

I pull away from him, and he steps down the row of barely-there wooden pegs pounded into hard dirt. I don't like thinking about sleeping down here. It's too dark and tiny, and it's like the walls are compressing my lungs. Plus, I don't know how D-39 will fit.

On one wall, six rows of shelves give splinters for free and canned goods are stored alphabetically. Top row: baga stew, corn, grapesquash. On the third row: meatscramble, home-preserved glass jars full of panchobeans. Bottom row: rice.

On the side wall: Stacked silver drums of water. Enough for one month, no longer. At least we *hope* it's enough. There's really no way to tell.

Tell

Papa nods as he admires the place. *This makes more sense to me than Dr. Tannin's plan.* His words are soft, like he's talking to himself and forgot that I'm even here.

I crease my brow. This could be my chance to get more information. *The sleeping plan?* He cups his hand against his ear like he didn't hear me. *Say again?* He looks just like a comedian in an old show we watched together years ago on the streamscreen. That's how I know he *did* hear me. *It's not for you to worry about.*

I shrug away from him, refusing to snicker-giggle like I might have a year ago. He never tells me anything these days. He shuffles around, counting, measuring, taking stock. *Hmmm,* he says, patting one shelf, then the other. I suck in my breath as he runs his hands under the cot. When his fingers find the hideyhole, I know what's coming. *Klynt, where is the other can of m-fuel?*

I swallow, remembering the day D-39 came to the Anchor T. What I did to save my robo. And what I've had to do about ten times since. It's true that robos guzzle m-fuel. It really is. *I don't know.* His eyes are anger-slits. *Don't lie to me, girl.* I straighten. Just "girl." No "sugar."

Gone, I tell him. *All used up.* My heart thud-jams against my ribs as we stare at each other. The burrow is silent, so silent. Until D-39 shatters the moment with a bark. *Arf!* Papa and I both jump, but Papa recovers first, realization bigskying his eyes. *Bring the D-39 and meet me in the truck. Right now. We're going to the pit. There'll be no more messing around.*

Messing Around

Papa sits behind the wheel tall and straight as a grain silo. He doesn't speak to me the whole way.

D-39 rides beside me, his head propped on the open window, nose thrust into the blusterblow, bandana rippling. Peeking out from the underside of the scratchpatched ear are a few silky hairs. I check the other ear, and it's there, too. So soft! Dog Alive sure went all out on the D-39 model. I mean, the fur lining the ears isn't just silky, it's warm, too.

To think I might never have known that, if not for this ride to the salvage pit. I stroke his ears. *You're full of surprises, aren't you?* I hardpress back tears as my robo keeps messing around, licking the wind. Why couldn't I have discovered this sooner? What other things will I never learn about him?

Because these are my last moments with D-39. I know what Papa will do at the pit. He will trade my robo for m-fuel.

For M-Fuel

Mama wouldn't allow this trade. I know she wouldn't. D-39's value can't be measured. But what can I do right here, right now to be a hero, to be like Mama?

We drive down deserted, dirtdusty roads, careful to go the right speed so we don't waste any more m-fuel. I squeeze D-39 tight. I swear I hear a heartbeat and can feel his breath rising and falling. Even though I know it's just the stupid truck bouncing me toward a certain future.

Future

When we get to the pit I have to make my legs easyeasy when what I want is to dashlong away from the old metal barn. I don't want D-39 sold off for parts. I want him whole. Beside me.

D-39 trots along, tail waving like a flag. He doesn't have any idea why we're here. He trusts me, and I'm now leading him to be salvaged. No matter how slowly I walk, D-39 stays at exactly my pace. Because it's what I've trained him to do.

My chest ripclaws. All that training, for what?

Inside we find Gloria wearing coveralls and a headband magnifier, tinkering with a box of spare robo parts. She's half farmer, half scientist, and half something from the future. Today I'm no good at fractions.

When Papa tells her why we've come, she nods. *Glad you caught me. I'm just back from a delivery up north, and some desperadoes were in here this morning, unloading some pretty good stuff. I paid them off in currency, so I can't help you if that's what you're after.*

Papa shakes his head. *Don't need currency. We're here to trade.*

Trade

My shoulders slump as Gloria lifts D-39 onto her worktable. His tail swishswipes like she's a friend.

I turn away. Stupid robo. Can't even tell when someone is going to dismantle him for parts.

Gloria examines D-39, running her hand along his back and belly. He flinches when she taps around his scratchpatched ear with her screwdriver. Gloria's eyebrows jagsaw. *Strange.* She shines a penlight into D-39's eyes, and his eyelids shutterbug as he pulls away. Gloria's eyes lock on mine for the briefest moment—so fast I'm almost not sure it happened. My breath catches. She's about to tell us something terrible, I just know it.

She uses the penlight to illuminate D-39's chestplate. *It's a Dog Alive, all right. See?* The light shines on the label I already know by heart. *It's got the logo, stamp, and encryption, but there's something odd about it.* Gloria focuses on Papa now. *Could be a fancied-up model. Or military.* She shrugs.

Or could be just a glitch. She pats D-39's head. *Not sure I'd trade this one, Link. Might fetch a better price from a robo junkie who deals in working machines. This one's too special.*

Special

I rest my nose against the warm metal. *D-39*, I croon, and when he licks me it's full on my mouth. And I can't help it: I snickergiggle. *You're a special slipslop is what you are.*

Papa's cheeks lift, and for a second I think he's going to snickergiggle, too. Instead he turns to Gloria. *Military, huh?* She shrugs. *Maybe.* Papa shoves his hands in his pockets. *What about a manual? I'd like to read up on him before I decide.*

Gloria shuffles through a filebox once, twice. *Sorry, no manual.* She opens a drawer and ruffles some papers. *But I do have this.* She hands Papa what looks like an old Dog Alive sales flyer advertising several robos, including the D-39 model. I scan the text.

Programmed with the latest learning software.

Make this robo the dog of your dreams!

D-39

NEW! Solar/m-fuel hybrid comes complete with more than 200 lifelike movements, expressions, and sounds • Luxurious faux fur—choose your color • 100% trainable—will respond to verbal commands • Waterproof • Drinks and wets • Eats and poops

 **12 Breeds** NOW AVAILABLE

DOG 🐾 ALIVE
Real as a dog can be!™

NO ASSEMBLY REQUIRED

Required

I lift my eyes from the flyer. I don't need to read these words, not really. Because I already know how amazing my robo is. D-39 *is* the dog of my dreams. He really is. So I make my case, because that's what this situation requires. *See, Papa, I told you he* is *special. And if we keep him, I could train him to do even more things, like be useful on the farm. Look how much he's learned already! He could be a workdog* and *a pet. He could earn his keep.* When I grab his hand, Papa shakes his head. I brace myself for the no.

No

No one is more zapjawed than me when Papa pulls the envelope of medical supplies from his backpack. Medical supplies he got from Dr. Tannin. *What about this?* he asks Gloria. *What's it worth?*

She quirkfaces. *For this I can give you three cans of m-fuel. I'll even throw in a box of ammo.* Papa holds out his hand and they shake. *Then we'll keep the D-39.*

Right then and there, my heart stops. Keep D-39! It's a yes, not a no! Before I even know what I'm doing, I throw myself against Papa. *Thank you, thank you, thank you! Papa, you're the best!*

The Best

I'm not sure about the best, Gloria teases. Her eyebrows narrow as she again examines D-39's chestplate. She opens her mouth to say something when the barn door swings open. Papa tenses and keeps a hand heavy on my shoulder as a robopatrol of three enters. I know what Papa's communicating to me: Stay calm and quiet. Be ready.

Gloria puts her hands flat on the counter. It's best to show submissiveness to robo-soldiers right away. *Can I help you?* The patrol separates, and each strides in a different direction. *Routine surveillance*, the leader says. *Well then*, Gloria says, turning her attention back to us. *Now that we're settled up, you can be on your way.* Papa and Gloria exchange a look, and I command D-39 to stay close as we leave the building, our m-fuel cans tucked in a paper sack. *Pleasure doing business*, Papa calls. *Thanks*, Gloria replies. *Come again soon.*

Outside we hurry to the truck, and Papa cranks it and puts it in gear. But we don't leave right away. *We'll wait until they're gone*, Papa says. *To be sure Gloria is safe.* I nod, gripping D-39's neckfur. I don't take a full breath until we see the patrol come out, and Gloria gives an everything's-okay nod from the doorway. Within seconds we are easing out of the parking lot like it's a regular day.

Regular Day

Mama, I hope you're listening. D-39 is mine. For keeps! I want everyone to know, especially Jopa. As we jerkjolt in the truck toward the Anchor T, I scan the Dog Alive flyer again. *Get this, Papa. D-39 is water-proof! Can you believe it?* Papa shrugs. *At this point, I'll believe anything.* He shakes his head. I wait for him to say something about the robopatrol, but he doesn't. *Maybe when we get home you can introduce him to the creek? Catch us some fish for supper?* His voice is back to his regular voice, and my breathing is normal again. My stomach grumbles at the thought of a fish dinner.

As soon as we get home I grab my pole, and D-39 bounds out after me, red bandana flashing, on our way to the creek.

The Creek

The sun warms my back as we hike past the looganuts, D-39 at my heel, like I taught him. The soft gurgle of the water against the sandy bank reaches us before we see it, and D-39's ears perk. I stroke his back as he noses my thigh. *Pretty, isn't it?*

At the creek bank, D-39 sits beside me as I slip off my shoes. I scan the fields for Jopa, hoping he'll show up, as he often does. It's like he has a radar for wherever I am.

Go on, I say to D-39. *You can get in.* I guess he doesn't know he's waterproof, because he doesn't. He paces alongside the water, paws never close enough to get wet. *You don't like the water?* I rub his neck. *It's okay. It feels good.* I slip my feet in to show him. D-39 only paces, whines.

Come on, I tell him, and I wade in. The water is cool on my legs, but not cold. After a jinglesnap I sink so low that only my shoulders and head show, even though the water's only about waist deep. I crouch in the middle of the creek, my feet careful on the sharp rocks as my arms flow with the current.

Current

The water curls around me, silky, like
Mama's robe—the floral one that still
hangs in the back of Papa's closet. I flip
onto my back to float downstream a bit.
D-39 barks, and next thing I know, he's
in the water, legs pumping as if he's been
swimming forever. His teeth clamp gently
onto my shoulder—sharp, firm—and I
realize he thinks I'm sinking. He thinks
I'm drowning!

My robo pulls me toward the shore, legs
motoring like jayballs. *Good boy*, I croon.
I don't resist a bit as he drags me safely to
the shore. And there's Jopa waiting for us,
ant jar in hand. *Wow*, he says. *D-39 saved
your life*. I quirkface. *I know*. No one has to
tell me that an ordinary robodog wouldn't
have done that.

Papa's letting me keep him, I tell Jopa.
Forever? Jopa asks. When I nod, he whoops,
and we both rub D-39 all over. I lean into
my robo. My D-39. *You are special*, I sweetmurmur, and I scratch under his chin. Not
that I needed Gloria or Jopa or anyone to
tell me that. *Such a good boy.*

Good Boy

When I tell Papa about what D-39 did at the creek, he nods. *Never heard of a robo doing that. No telling what his story is, where he's been.* I quirkface. *He could be a spy.* I'm joking, but the way Papa's face darkens, I know he's taking my words seriously. *He's definitely a watcher.* He gently nudges my shoulder. *Like you.* A tiny quirk rearranges his lips.

After that I notice how D-39 studies a pair of swallows making their nest in the eaves where the gutter bends. One afternoon when a flock of flying robofighters roars overhead, I startle, my heart about to rammerjammer out of my chest. But D-39 doesn't shrink or chase, simply follows with his eyes. As if he's trying to learn how to fly.

How to Fly

Run! shouts Papa, arms shooshooing me
forward like a goose teaching a fledgling
how to lift off the water. But the sky clears
almost as soon as the words are out of his
mouth. His eyes narrow as he searches for
more planes. But there's nothing but blue.
Get inside the house, he snarls.

I do, and Papa strides across the yard. He
kicks the sandbox out of the way, throws
the hatch, and disappears inside the burrow
for a long time.

A Long Time

When I ask Papa about it later, he doesn't answer me right away, and he won't look me in the eye. I don't have any idea why Papa is avoiding me, but I notice that he's carrying both his guns now—even the rifle, which used to stay locked in the case under his bed. *I'm not sure*, he says finally. *Maybe nothing. Probably the government doing surveillance. Nothing that hasn't happened before, but now they're intimidating us with planes instead of drones.* His voice has a quiverquake in it that I've heard only when he tells the story of Mama's death. I don't know what that quiverquake means. Fear? Sorrow? Is Papa lying to me?

My fingers curl around D-39's good ear as I work to steady my heart. I stroke the top of his head for a long time before I unknot the red bandana. We don't need anything that might draw attention. Because it seems to me those flying robofighters showing up on a blue afternoon are the opposite of *nothing*.

Nothing

I'm about to say something when Jopa—
little Jopa—barrels into the yard. *Did you
see them?* he asks, breathless.

D-39 prancedances with excitement, so I
hold him by the collar. He loves Jopa, but
I don't want him to knock the kid over. *I
saw them*, I say.

Well? he asks. I bite my lip and realquick
glance at Papa. His eyes warn me to not
alarm Jopa by sharing any of our theories,
which may or may not be correct. It's true
that Jopa is my best—only—playmate, but
he's still so young. He deserves to feel safe
and protected for as long as possible. *Well,
nothing,* I say.

Jopa takes a breath, then drops to his
knees and wraps his arms around D-39. My
robo nuzzles Jopa's pocket until a candy
wrapper drops out. *Oops*, Jopa says. *That
was from my breakfast.* We both watch as
D-39 licks the wrapper, pushing it around
the ground with his tongue. *He likes it*, I
say. I can't imagine any robo having better

smell receptors than D-39. I wonder if that's one of his souped-up, military features that Gloria mentioned at the pit.

I love my ants, Jopa says. *But sometimes I wish I had a dog.* D-39 flops onto the floor beside him, and Jopa rubs D-39's barrel of a belly as if they have always been friends.

Friends

After that we spot flying robofighters every day, all through the month. We see Jopa every day, too, because he slips away from home when Tiev is supposed to be watching him while their mother works. It's easy for him to leave unnoticed because Tiev has other priorities than entertaining her little brother. *It's humdrum*, Jopa says. *All Tiev wants to do is push-ups and jogging in place.*

I like having Jopa around. We hang out together and talk, like friends. I can tell by Papa's droopbottom face that he doesn't like playing a part in Jopa's disobedience, but he never tells him to go home. I nudge Jopa's shoulder to make him quirkface. *It's humdrum here, too.*

No it's not, he says. *You've got D-39.* I can't help it: I quirkface. Jopa's right. By some miracle, I don't have time to lament not-yet-found pieces for my Museum of Fond Memories. I still tinker—I can't not tinker—but I get outside more. Even the looganut chores don't bother me the way they used to. All because I have D-39.

D-39

One day I wake up and D-39 isn't beside me. My heart thudjams. *Papa,* I call. *Have you seen D-39?*

No answer. I throw open the door and race onto the porch and down the steps. *D-39! Come!* I scan the area, wishing not for the first time that he still wore the red bandana, so I could spot him more easily— thanks a lot, flying robofighters. No matter how much I holler, D-39 doesn't come. Papa doesn't answer either. But that's not unusual. Unless the blusterblow is just right, it can be hard to hear anything from one side of the farm to the other.

What's unusual is no D-39. No D-39 any- where. I don't know what to do. I'm fast falling into panic mode. And then Mama's voice comes to me: *Go to Jopa's.*

I race down the road and don't stop until I see Jopa's house. Parked in front is the broken-down blue truck that hides the hatch to the Tannins' shelter. Scattered all around the front of the truck is a bunch of trash. I recognize dozens of those little chocolate nub wrappers like the one in Jopa's pocket, and there's also my robo— bright and golden as looganuts in bloom.

In Bloom

As soon as his sensors detect me, D-39 lifts his head, and I see that he's been tearing into the trash heap. Now he's licking an empty can of who-knows-what. *D-39*, I scold, and he swishswipes that plumy tail like a jayballed ticktock pendulum, face radiating happiness. He's so pleased with his prize that instead of cursing the programmers the way Papa would, I watch that tail, and I can feel the quirk blooming across my face. How can I shout at him? I can't. Instead I pat his head and pick up the trash.

Trash

Before long Jopa flies out of his house like he's fleeing a tornado. I'm not alarmed, because that's how he does most everything—at full tilt. Jopa doesn't fussfidget about what D-39 has done, he only quirkfaces his gappy quirk. *Hey*, he says, and lifts a rainbow skysail with a hole in the middle from the heap. *This isn't trash.* He hands it to me like it's an injured bird, then sets off looking for the ball of string.

The hole is actually a T-shaped cut, like the skysail got caught on a branch or the corner of the house. *You can fix it*, I hear my mother say. I turn it over in my hand, remembering the fat roll of duct tape under the cot in our burrow. *Want to try and fix it?* I ask, because I'm sure I can.

Really? Jopa says. *We can make it fly?* I nod. *But first let's clean up after D-39.* Jopa says okay and sidles up to me sweet as D-39, and his face is as pure and untroubled as a hotseason sunset.

Sunset

Another rations day, another month.

The air turns brisk, as it does in leafseason, but we still take our supper on the porch. Papa sits beside me, pipe between his teeth, but no smoke, because the tobacco has run out. We pump the swing back and forth with our feet, D-39 half in my lap, half hanging off. If I didn't know better, I'd swear my robo had gained weight.

When one of D-39's fat paws gets caught between the slats, Papa reaches to free it. But D-39 misunderstands and snags Papa's hand with his teeth. Papa curses, and D-39 leaps away, the bite mark on Papa's hand a half moon rising.

Rising

The first thing I hear when I wake the next morning is the emergency broadcast siren and a solid *click*. Then nothing.

My heart rammerjammers as I hurry into the kitchen, D-39 behind me. Papa clears his throat and shakes his head. *I can't believe it.*

What's wrong? I say. He's standing at the counter crushing looganuts with a mortar and pestle instead of using the grinder.

His eyelids shutterbug. *Power's out.* His voice is calm, even. Like it's no big deal. *Loogabutter will be chunky today.* He backs away from the counter and brushes his hands. *Why don't you finish up? I'll be in the field.*

It takes a minute, but after Papa is gone, the news of the blackout settles over me like a net. I think about what it could mean: more flying robofighters or boomblasts. *Here.* Panic rises inside me, making my hands twitch—that's how much I need to be doing something. But then I see the skysail. The broken skysail I promised to fix for Jopa, and I remember my mission.

Mission

I pretend I'm a wolf, a scout stalking likely prey. I sneak past the swing set, D-39 beside me as always, and I push away the sandbox and lift the hatch.

The metal creaks, and the hatch is heavier than I remember. But I keep tugging, and finally we both fall backward onto the ground. I ramscramble down the pegs, lungs filling with the earth-scented air. I flick the lantern on, even though it isn't all that bright. My hand pats the dirt under the cot, past the stack of ammo and batteries and m-fuel hideyhole until I find the fat roll of tape. I slip my fingers into the center and wear it like a bracelet as I climb up and out into sunlight.

Sunlight

Papa doesn't come in for lunch, so I crank open a jar of panchobeans. They taste bright, crisp, like the sun during the first days of hotseason. D-39 stretches out on the floor at my feet, watching the spoon move from the jar to my mouth. Next thing I know, he's snoring.

The house feels strangely calm all shadowed and dark, like the way it feels sometimes before a cold-duststorm. I finish my half of the beans and leave the rest for Papa. I fussfidget for a little while with the tape since there are other uses for it in my Museum of Fond Memories. When an hour passes and Papa *still* doesn't come in, I sit down with the book I recently started. I try, but I can't read. I'm too keyed up.

Keyed Up

I lift the one photograph of Mama from its place on the mantel and stroke its tarnished frame. *Hey hi ho there.* Mama and Papa on their wedding day, so smooth-faced and young, before Mama started the K-9 Corridor. Before me.

I study her face. The dimple in her left cheek is the twin of mine. I scan her hair, her body, everything. My heart thudjams the way it does every time I look at this picture. If she died the way Papa says she did—in border crossfire—then why have I never heard about it? It was never reported on the streamscreen. No mention of it in any newsource, ever.

I mean, I'm sure there've been unreported deaths at the border. Lots of them. And many more have died trying to get there. It's an unforgiving landscape, heavily patrolled. You have to know where the gaps are, where to sneak across. But if it had been Ersu Tovis, veterinarian and hero to all living, breathing dogs, someone somewhere would have made the news of her death public.

I stroke her face. *Are you listening, Mama? I know you're out there.* She's out there, and she wants to come home to me. But something—someone—is holding her back. I'm certain of it. When D-39 whines, I set down the photo and rub him all over. *Want to go play fetch?*

Fetch

I carry the skysail in one hand and in the other a ball to toss for D-39. The water's too cold now for me to put more than a finger in, but it doesn't bother D-39. He swims out for the flung tennis ball like he was never startlespooked by the water.

He holds his head high, and I can almost see his legs churning, but not quite. When he strikes and snags the ball with his teeth, his head lifts impossibly higher. As I examine my skysail handiwork, I too am filled with pride.

Pride

For a jinglesnap I forget about the blackout. All I can think about is showing Jopa the skysail, because I'm pretty sure I've not only fixed it but improved it. I call D-39 and the water runs in rivulets down his shiny plates. He shakes and rolls in the dirt, his polka-dotted tongue lolling out of his quirkfacing mouth. We hike to Jopa's house, where D-39 announces us with a sharp bark. Within seconds Tiev cracks open the door. *Sorry, Klynt*, she says. *Jopa's grounded for raiding the chocolate stash. He can't come out right now.*

I have to stop myself from quirkfacing, because of course Jopa raided the chocolate stash. He was probably feeding his ants. I hold out the skysail. *He can't come out even for this?* Jopa peeps from behind his sister. *Please, Tiev?* When Tiev rolls her eyes, I know the yes is coming. *Okay*, she says in a humdrummed voice. *Go ahead.* I realize in those three syllables that Tiev probably feels about caring for Jopa all the time the same way I do about looganuts.

Jopa whoops and cruises out the door, where D-39 greets him with tailswipes and happy licks to his hands. Jopa's eyes bigsky as I hand him the skysail. *Does it work?* I shrug. *Let's find out.* D-39 follows as I walk backward, unraveling the string. *Ready?* I ask. When Jopa lifts the skysail, I start running.

Running

I feel it the instant the blusterblow grabs the fabric—I don't even have to look back, but I do. The skysail is soaring high now, and D-39 barks as he runs beside me, all panting and quirkfacing like it's the best day ever.

Is this what it feels like to be a hero? This swelling in my chest as I look at Jopa and D-39?

Higher, Jopa shouts. I let some more string out and slow to a walk. I don't have to run anymore—the blusterblow has it, and all I have to do is hold on. For the longest, most perfect moment, the skysail glides, and I hear my mother whispering, *Fly, Klynt, fly.*

Fly

I'm not sure which sound I hear first: Tiev hollering for Jopa or the flock of robo-fighters beelining toward us. Flying not high in the sky like before, but so close you can touch them.

As Tiev drags Jopa toward their house, I think for a second it might be safer to follow them in, but then my mind whip-whirls to Papa. What if he needs me?

I drop the skysail string to cover my ears, and I run with D-39 homehomehome. Back to Papa.

Papa

He waves his arms, shouts, *Klynt, Klynt, Klynt!* And I know I did the right thing leaving Jopa's and coming back to the Anchor T. Papa's eyes are wild—like a prairie fire in a blusterblow. When another boomblast falls somewhere close behind us it thudjams my eardrums as I runrunrun, and Papa grabs me up and throws me over his shoulder, even though I'm too big for that. He carries me past the swing set, to the sandbox, and into the open hatch.

Hatch

Just before the metal slams out sunlight,
D-39 noses himself safely through the
hatch, like I knew he would. I grab his
collar so he doesn't tumble down the peg
steps, but he's so heavy it only ends up
pulling us both down until we're on the
hard ground.

D-39 ramscrambles to his feet, and I touch
my nose to his nose, feel his body quiverquake as the blackness swallows us. The
cans on the shelves fatrattle with each
blast, and I cover my head, waiting to be
buried alive.

Alive

Somehow I end up hardpressed against Papa's chest, so close that I can smell sweat and feel the porcupine of his beard on my forehead. We stay that way until the boomblasts get less frequent and they sound farther away. Only then do we untangle as Papa pulls the lantern from beneath his cot and flicks it on to reveal the air alive with specks of dirtdust. Papa's brows go jayballs as he tracks D-39's every pace and whine. Like D-39 is the enemy.

Enemy

Anytime there's an explosion above us, D-39 lifts his ears and paces, whines. Paces, whines some more. I stroke his scratchpatched ear, not sure if the comfort is more for me or him. *It's okay, D-39. We're safe down here. The enemy can't get us.* Papa pries my arms off my robo. *Let him fussfidget. Must be part of his programming. We'll watch and listen to the D-39, and we'll know whether or not we should worry.*

Worry

Sometimes D-39 paces and whines when Papa and I don't hear a thing happening above. *It's like he's our alarm system*, I say.

A hungry *alarm system*, Papa says, and his mouth forms a hard line. I ignore him, because it's not news that D-39 guzzles m-fuel *and* regular food. That's the way the Dog Alive company made him. I switch my thoughts to Jopa. *Papa, do you think Jopa's okay?* He's quiet for a long moment. *We made it, didn't we?*

The hair on the back of my neck prickle-twitches. Yes, we did make it, but that doesn't mean Jopa did. I just wish I knew. Was Tiev prepared enough to get them from their house to their burrow? Between the skysail and the first boomblast on his front lawn, there wasn't much more time than a jinglesnap.

Jinglesnap

The burrow is so dark we wouldn't even know what time it is if not for the tick-tock Papa hung on the wall right above the drums of water. Each moment is a jingle-snap and endless at the same time. The underground air is cool, and not a speck of light shows through the hatch. It's like being inside a nutshell. No VCR in progress, no printing press. No pile of wires and metal for me to tinker with. And no ham.

I miss the ham already, or maybe what I miss more is the possibility it holds, even though so far no one has ever radioed me back. Papa and I hardly talk. We listen to the strange music of what's happening above us. Every time we think the boomblasts have stopped, that the attack is over, we hear another one, or D-39 reacts to something we can't hear. My heart runs on overdrive, all my senses on high alert. I don't dare tell Papa about Jopa and me flying that bright, here-we-are skysail.

Skysail

I'm startlespooked that he'll say it's my fault we're in the burrow. I sink my hands into my pockets and shift as far away from Papa as I can.

If only I had thought before I let that flash of rainbow climb into the air. It was like telling the robofighters, *Aim here!* And now here we are, stuck.

Stuck

Finally the ticktock says it's bedtime so I lie in my cot and stare at the lantern-lit faces smiling from the food labels, a reminder of what lives and grows in our colorful world—our world that's turning to gray rubble with every boomblast. *Papa, how long do you think we'll have to stay down here?* His eyes find my eyes in the dim light. *As long as it takes.* It's another one of Papa's many answers that's not really an answer.

Answer

I ignore Papa, shut out the sound of boomblasts, and wrap myself around D-39. As the shapes and shadows of our few belongings flicker in the lantern-light, I make patterns and designs in my mind. Like finding elephants and dragons hiding in the clouds. I'm too panicky to be hungry, and when I finally do get to sleep, I dream of Everlake—Mama's answer and my favorite dream.

Dream

The Wilds. Moose and bears and wolves and jays hiding in the leafgiants as Mama and I skate on the ice-sparkle lake, spinning and snickergiggling, spinning and snicker-giggling. Dogs of different kinds chase and quirkface. Even D-39 is there. Until a blade of cold air finds my face, and I wake up gasping.

Gasping

The hatch is cracked, and Papa's muscles are straining, eyes squintchecked, cheeks ruddy as he pushes D-39 out.

I bolt off the cot, grab Papa's legs. *No!* I scream, and pull him away from the pegs. It's enough to knock Papa off balance, and he tumbles with D-39 to the floor.

They thump onto the hard dirt, and my chest throbs as I pull D-39 to me. *How could you?* Papa knows how I feel about D-39. He knows my robo is not just a machine to me. Sobs shake Papa's body and his eyes are wet and shiny. He wraps me in his arms, kisses my hair, my eyelids, my ears. *Klynt, I'm sorry. So, so sorry.* He squeezes me tighter than he ever has. I wish we lived in a different world.

Different World

Now my hands curl around D-39's scratch-patched ear day and night. Even after Papa explains to me it isn't only about D-39's hunger. *I think they're looking for robos, sugar girl. Remember when Gloria said he might be military? I think he really is a spy or something. He could be the reason we got boomblasted.*

Boomblasted

I shake my head. I won't believe it, can't believe it. *It was the skysail. Not D-39.* D-39 is mine. He wouldn't do anything to hurt me. Papa's eyes squintcheck. *What skysail?* I clamp my mouth shut, and I get that prickletwitchy feeling again. *It was for Jopa,* I explain.

I wait for it, but Papa doesn't curse or sigh or anything. He doesn't say another word. I soothe myself by stroking the silky inside of D-39's scratchpatched ear. The silence is far worse than anything Papa might say.

I try to sleep with one eye open, but it doesn't work. My chest fistclenches whenever I remember the skysail and the boomblasts and the running and Papa trying to push D-39 up and out.

Sure Papa might have relented this time, but what about the next time he gets startlespooked? There's nothing changed about our situation. All Papa's reasons to get rid of D-39 are still valid. My heart nosedives when I imagine life without my dog—a life of darkness.

Darkness

Without sunlight, it's hard to know when to wake. But by the sixth day, we have a set routine: Papa shakes me until I swing my legs off the cot. We eat loogameal for breakfast, and D-39 whines just like a real dog.

We use a bucket for a poopflush and add a layer of kitty litter each time. I pinch my nose to null the odor, but the place still reeks, even with the so-tight lid.

We watch the ticktock, listen for boomblasts. I try to read, but my eyes dart and my mind skips. Will I ever get to finish restoring the old typewriter? Will I ever broadcast again on the ham? I get a crick in my neck from always looking up.

Looking Up

By the second week the boomblasts are less frequent and sometimes I can read a whole chapter in one sitting. Papa has let me mark the wall with my screwdriver each morning so we can keep count of the days. *Only one more week until rations day,* he says. *One more week until the cease-fire.* He chews the end of his pipe. *If it's safe, we'll go up then.*

Safe—such a strange word. I no longer know what it means.

What It Means

Each day that passes, our trash heap
grows along with the stench. So many
empty cans! Thanks to D-39's polka-dotted
tongue they're all perfectly sparkshined.
Papa says that's what real dogs do, but I
never read that in Mama's books. *How do
you know?* I ask, and between boomblasts
he tells me about a dog he had as a kid.
Named Sounder, he says. *After the book.*
Another dog he and Mama had, named
Lassie, was named after a retro book and a
show on the streamscreen. His voice turns
thick when he tells me Lassie died of BrkX.

The part of all this I can't believe is how
different Papa is without the fields to run
to. He still stays busy all the time—reading
aloud from books, sharpening our knives,
teaching me—but he's not humpgrumped
about it. Not so distracted by everything
that needs to be done. Sometimes he even
seems joyslammed. *Today,* he says, after I
mark the wall with the screwdriver for the
thirteenth time, *let's talk about how to tie
a bowline.*

How to Tie a Bowline

Papa hands me a six-foot piece of nylon rope. *This knot is your number one go-to rescue knot.* I'm not sure who Papa thinks I'll be rescuing, but I don't ask. *Think of a rabbit,* he says. I pull the slick rope across my palm. *A real rabbit or a roborabbit?*

Neither, he says. *Think of the shoelace rabbit.* I lift my eyebrow. I probably wouldn't have learned to tie my shoes without that rabbit. *Yes. Except this rabbit is a shy rabbit.* He quirkfaces. Actually quirkfaces. *Like you. And me, sometimes.*

He shows me: rabbit comes out of the hole, around the leafgiant, and back in the hole. It takes all day but when I finally get it, the knot doesn't slip.

Slip

By the twentieth day, I'm so humdrummed of being cooped up I don't want anything touching me, not even D-39. Our shelves are mostly bare, and if I have to eat one more panchobean I think I will scream and never stop.

Meanwhile, Papa is calm as anything. None of his emotions slips out of his mouth today. *Tomorrow*, he says, and whittles bits of wood into chess pieces. He's talking about rations day. If there still is a rations day.

What if we hear boomblasts? I ask. *God willing, we won't*, Papa says, his jaw quiver-quaking. *We have to go up, Klynt. Be the heroes of our own story. Survivors try.*

Try

I throw a blanket over me and D-39 to block
out Papa and the ticktock and the stink.
I pretend I'm Noah watching the animals
board the ark, two by two. I see elephants
and lions and panda bears and real golden
retrievers. No computer chips, no wires, no
motors.

I batten the hatches and steer the ship to
a place where dogs run and play, and robos
are nothing but toys. To a place where it is
always dawn.

Dawn

Rations day. Papa quirkfaces when he shakes my cereal out of the box. *Ready?*

All I can do is nod. *It's going to be fine*, Papa says as he loads a pack. Since we can't predict what the world will be like, he says we should bring all the most important stuff with us. He hardpresses matches, rope, cotton balls, a bedsheet, and our water filter into his pack before handing me a book for us to read, D-39's m-fuel, and lip balm. *Got your screwdriver? Your slingshot?*

I pat for them, and they are right where they are supposed to be. As Papa climbs the pegs, I keep one eye on him and one eye on D-39. I am always on guard.

On Guard

D-39's tail stops swishswiping. His hackles rise. He paces. Whines. Growls just like a wild dog.

Wild Dog

The world inside the burrow stops as Papa
pops D-39's snout, and we train our ears up
and out into the air we can't see.

I grab Papa around the waist as something—a truck, maybe, a tank—rumbles
overhead, fatrattling the bag of empty
cans. Dirt shivers down the walls as we
hear a voice shout, *Quadrant one, clear!*
Inspecting quadrant two.

D-39's growls turn to snarls, and even
though I shush him, he barks. *Arf, arf, arf,*
arf! And he won't stop.

Stop

The rumbling-rattling-shivering stops as suddenly as it began. Papa's eyes meet mine as he palms D-39's chestplate. *No wonder.* He fingers the frayed tape over my robo's speakers. *Needs a fresh layer of tape.*

I don't have to look, because I already know the tape is frayed. I've known for days, maybe more than a week. I swallow. May as well get it over with. *There's no tape.* Because I took it out of the burrow to fix the skysail. Left it in my museum. But no way am I bringing that up. Not now.

Papa lets his eyelids close and a long breath comes out of his nose, all disappointment and resignation.

Hey hi ho there. Mama, if you're listening, I probably don't have to tell you that Papa's look is worse than a scolding. Because we both know that whoever is up there is waiting, listening.

Listening

There's one thing I can do. I ramscramble away, yank the blanket from the cot and wrap it around D-39's head to cover his sensors and speakers. And that's when I notice something odd. Right near D-39's scratchpatched ear is a piece of metal that's curling up, creating a crevice in the metal. I do not want my robo to start coming apart! I run my finger along the crevice, listening as much as touching. I don't find slick metal as I expected. Instead I find more fur.

D-39 is like a layer cake. Nothing about him is simple.

Simple

I tie the blanket in a simple knot, and Papa nods his approval. *Shhh*, I sweetmurmur and rub my nose to D-39's moist robo nose. I babytalk D-39, and he shifts from barking to gently licking my face.

I wonder if a real dog's tongue feels as slipsloppy as D-39's. Probably not, but what do I know? A real dog's tongue may be even more slipsloppy. Not that it even matters—what matters is that for now D-39 is quiet.

Quiet

I want to cheer when the motor above
us cranks and the truck or whatever it is
moves on.

Papa looks at the ticktock and frowns.
We can't wait. My whole body quiverquakes.
But there are soldiers up there. What I
mean is, I don't want another boomblast.
He waves his hand at the dirtdusty, bare
shelves. *We can't miss rations day.*

I can't stop my fingers shuddershaking as I
shoulder my pack. We're really doing this.
As D-39 pulls free of the blanket, I listen
for Mama's voice, but I don't hear it.

So it's not just me. The trucks have made
all of us startlespooked.

Startlespooked

At first I don't think the hatch will open.
Papa hardpresses and twists, but it doesn't
budge. *The tanks*, he says. *The boomblasts.
Probably made the ground settle, and now
it's ramjammed.*

He bangs around, making a racket far
worse than D-39's barking. I sit with my
arms around my robo, watching until my
neck aches from all that looking up.

Suddenly the burrow feels even smaller,
like it's shrinking around me, and my arms
itch, and all I can think about is getting
out. *What if we can't get out?* I say aloud,
without meaning to.

Klynt. Papa glares at me. *You can't think like
that.* His voice turns gentle. *You know this.
The first step to getting out, sugar girl, is to
believe* you're getting out.

Getting Out

Finally the hatch gives. As Papa eases it open, the metal announces itself with a long squeal that makes D-39 whine.

It's okay, I tell him, even though I don't know if that's true. D-39 cocks his head and watches with me as the sliver of light becomes a whole pie of blue sky.

Sky

Papa peeps out, and I close my eyes as my lungs hurryscurry to suck in fresh air. When I open my eyes, Papa's face is grim, but the sky above him is clear. *It's like we're on a different planet*, he says. *What have they done to the Anchor T?* He sags against the wall of pegs, and I want to go to him, to say it's okay, but it's like my feet are bolted to the floor.

Not D-39. He looks up at Papa, at the circle of light, and barks. He prancedances with excitement, his nose quiverquaking with remembered scents and new ones he can't wait to investigate. The only direction to go now is up.

Up

We hoist D-39 out first. Papa is the muscle.
I mostly comfort with words. *It's okay,
D-39. Almost there.*

My heart fatrattles as he disappears outside the hatch while I am still inside.

Quick as a lizard I ramscramble up the pegs
as Papa warns, *Stay low. Robofighters might
be watching.*

Watching

As my face finds the sun and my body recalculates the earth, my head throbs and my eyes water. I inhale the cool, fresh air in one long breath, then another.

My nose burns as I breathe, but I don't mind. It's so much better than the stinky kitty-litter air in the burrow.

And then the world unfurls in ribbons of color: yellow-brown-black beneath a swath of blue. I can't help it: I stretch toward the sky, reach my hands up and up. That's how joyslammed I am to know it's still here, that no matter how cooped we were in the burrow, the sky survived.

The sky is still here, and so are we.

We

D-39 quirkfaces at me as he races and rolls like it's the best day ever. Papa secures the hatch, and I help him drag the smashed sandbox back on top. *Let's go*, he says. *But be careful. We don't know what's out here.*

I call D-39 to my side and gasp when I see the mangled swing set, the slide flattened into the ground. And when I see what's left of the house, I hurtle toward it, as if I can save it if I can get there fast enough. We are lucky we made it to the burrow, because the house is a giant pile of rubble, like the inside of the printing press the first day I found it. My Museum of Fond Memories, gone. That one precious photograph of Mama, destroyed. If only I'd had time to grab it the day of the big boomblast!

My legs turn to stone. I can't breathe. All my work, all my treasures—gone.

Klynt. Papa grabs my arm to slow me, his voice low and growly. *We need to slow down. Careful where you put your feet.*

Feet

As I follow the tank tracks across the flattened looganut stalks, I steer clear of jagged edges and bits of glass that might cut through my shoes. I pick my way across what looks more like a landfill than my yard.

I don't dare look at Papa's face. I can't take his pain when I am too busy with my own. Just twenty-one days in the burrow, and it's a whole new world.

New World

All the old landmarks gone: no silo or cockadoodle weather vane or mailbox or barn. Pasture dotted with stray pieces of metal. A car door, a bathtub that looks like it might have been ours, but I can't tell for sure. We stumble forward, bent on checking the remains of the house before heading to Jopa's.

Jopa. The prickletwitch on my neck stretches all the way down my back. We've always gone to rations day with the Tannins. Always. But who knows what—or who—we will find at their house?

My lips-mouth-throat quickly turn gritty and dry from thirst. I keep my screwdriver ready, in spite of the fact that my hands are quiverquaking.

Quiverquaking

I call to D-39, and he bounds back to me, pants, licks my fingers. He, too, is trying to find his bearings.

Papa and I don't speak as we follow the tank tracks, or when we first see the Tannins' house across the field. Because my whole body is shuddershaking, I don't trust my voice right now. Jopa's house isn't quite as annihilated as ours. More like a skeleton of black, sagging bones.

Bones

D-39 noses around, finds a pile of what looks like chicken bones. *D-39*, I call, and he snuffles, lopes back to us. *I know they have a burrow*, Papa says. *But I'm not sure how to get inside.* My brow creases. Is it possible that I know something Papa doesn't? *This way*, I say. And lead him to the broken-down blue truck.

Blue Truck

It isn't so much a truck as two wheels and a blue truck bed, now halfway crushed by a giant uprooted oak, deepdark and splintered.

The truck is blue like denim, faded in places. Blue like the sky in some famous painting by a painter whose name I can't remember. Blue like a dream of water.

Water

Suddenly I am so thirsty I could drain the creek. Papa quicksqueezes my hand and releases it just as quick. *How did you know?* I half quirkface. *Jopa,* I say. I'm itchy with the anticipation of seeing him. All this time I've wanted to see his face, to know he's okay. D-39 will be joyslammed, too.

We push off a few tree branches to lift the blue truck bed, which looks formidable, but really isn't anything more than a thin sheet of metal. The metal provides mangled cover for what's between the truck and the leaf-giant: a fancy hatch with knobs and clasps, like something from a submarine.

Papa knocks. No answer. So he knocks again. D-39 looks from me to Papa to the hatch, like we can't seriously want to go back inside now that we're finally out in the fresh air. I keep my hand on his collar so he doesn't bolt. When there's still no answer, Papa's eyes meet mine. *They've probably gone to rations day.* I finger D-39's faux fur. *Without us?* I ask.

Papa takes a breath. *How could they have known we'd come?* He pauses, and I want to say something about how weird it is that they wouldn't check on us the way we're checking on them. But I don't, because I know as well as anyone that the day the boomblasts came changed everything. *I bet they're fine,* Papa says. *But I don't want to leave without being sure.*

Sure

Papa's eyes bigsky as I rearrange buttons
and clasps to pull open the door, just the
way Jopa showed me. I shrug. *It's not
hard if you know how.* As the words leave
my mouth, I think that might be true of
everything.

Inside the burrow is completely different
from ours. It smells of lavender, not waste.
No pegs. A real staircase that even D-39
handles with ease. A table lamp with an
LED bulb. Water from a faucet, like in a real
house. *Hello?* Papa says as I flip a switch to
turn on the overhead lights. *Anyone home?*
My heartbeat whirs in my ears like one of
D-39's fans as we wait for a response. *Jopa?*
I say.

Silence. I stand in the center of the room
and turn all the way around. D-39 noses
every corner. That's when I notice the
closed curtain.

The Closed Curtain

I've only been inside the burrow once, the day before we flew the skysail and the boomblasts came. Jopa wanted to show me where his mother stored the chocolate nubs.

I glance at the cabinet above the sink, and my stomach whines. Then an image of what's behind the curtain flashes into my mind, and my fingers shake as I push between the hanging flaps of fabric. *Jopa?*

Jopa

He's stretched flat on his back on a cot, eyes closed. The kid must sleep as hard as he plays. I quirkface when I see the jar of ants on the side table.

But then my eyes find a row of vials and needles on the wall behind him. Tubes snake from a hanging bag of clear liquid all the way to his arm, where the needle is secured with a piece of white tape.

I shrink back. This isn't Jopa, this is some version of Frankenstein. It's like we've walked onto the set of a horror show.

Horror Show

I understand now. Sleeping through the deathstretch. Before it was just words, but now I have a real picture. Dr. Tannin wanted to keep Jopa alive. So the liquid calories coursing through the IV tubes are laced with medication to keep him asleep and prevent him from burning calories.

Jopa is not Frankenstein's monster. He's a little prince who's waiting for someone to break the spell.

Spell

First I pat D-39's head to give me courage. *I can do this.* He watches me, his brown eyes steady as anything. I glance back at the curtain to be sure Papa's not coming yet.

I touch Jopa's arm. He doesn't twitch or shutterbug, but his skin is reassuringly warm and whispersmooth. Oh so gently, I peel back the tape that holds in the needle. The skin beneath is puckered and bruised, like a row of purple humpbacks in a landscape painting. *I can do this*, I whisper again, like it's a magic spell. I take a breath and ease the needle out of Jopa's arm. I think of it like pulling weeds in the looganut fields—*easy, easy, firm.* My movements are deliberate and careful, so that root to leaf, the weeds remain unbroken.

Unbroken

I expect Jopa to pop up right away, but he doesn't. I watch his chest lift with each breath, so I know he's still alive. Jopa's whole and alive! But he's not Jopa, not like this. I stroke his arm. *Come on, Jopa.* D-39 bumps his head against my thigh. My robo must think I'm talking to him, or else he senses my anxiety and is trying to reassure me.

The curtain hangs smooth, unbroken until Papa pushes it open. He curses as he steps inside, and his fingers find the now-dangling tubes. *Oh Klynt, what have you done?*

Done

I had to, I say. *Jopa didn't want to sleep through the deathstretch.* Papa shakes his head, takes a deep breath. I wait for him to scold me, to say it wasn't for me to decide, because I know it wasn't. But what I'm learning is that in a deathstretch, all the rules that once seemed black and white are nothing but gray. Everything is upside down and turned around. It's like we're making up the rules as we go along.

For a jinglesnap I think Papa might insert the needle back into Jopa's vein. But he doesn't. *Well*, he says. *It's done now, isn't it? And we're running out of time. Dr. Tannin and Tiev are probably at rations day. If we don't go now, we'll miss it. We need food and supplies. We've got to go. It's our only chance.*

Only Chance

Jopa still isn't moving. *What about Jopa? I say. We can't just leave him here.* Papa runs his hands through his hair. *You're right. We can't leave him to wake up alone.* My eyes bigsky. *Maybe we can carry him,* I suggest. *D-39 could help.*

Papa shakes his head. *Klynt, it's too far with us traveling on foot. We'll never make it in time.* He drags a hand over his face, changing from troubled to certain. *If we're going to make it, we need to go right now, this moment.*

This Moment

My heart stalls, clicking like an engine that won't turn over. If we can't carry Jopa, and we can't leave him, what can we do? We need to go to rations day, obviously. And not just for the food. I need more sky to help make up for all those days in the burrow. *Please, Papa. D-39 can do this. We'll make a sling, and he can drag Jopa behind. You know he'll follow me anywhere. And I promise he'll be fast.*

Emotions stream across Papa's face as he turns to Jopa. *Look at him, Klynt.* His voice starts jagged, then turns sharp. *We can't move him. Not like this.* My throat aches, but my back straightens. It's my fault we're in this mess. First the skysail and now unplugging Jopa. This moment wouldn't be happening if not for my rash actions. I swallow hard. I know what I have to do, even though it makes my stomach fist-clench. *You go, Papa. I'll stay with Jopa. We can't leave him alone.*

Alone

Papa bends down and grabs my shoulders to look me in the eye. *You want to stay here? Alone?*

I shake my head. Of course I don't want to. But if I've learned anything from Mama it's that sometimes people have to do things they don't want to do. Because it's the right thing, the best thing. I swallow my desire to see the world, to see other people, to know what and who is left in our corner of the Worselands. That all disappears, quick as a rabbit into brush. I'm not sure if this makes me a hero or a fool. Do these words, these labels, really matter during a deathstretch?

I lift my chin, place my hand on D-39's warm, solid back. *Besides, I'm not alone.*

IV.

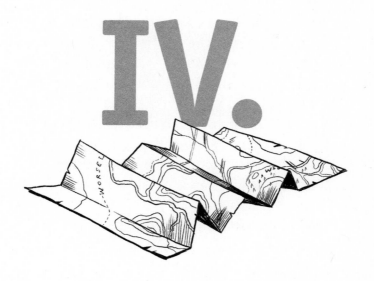

Not Alone

Papa rearranges his pack, moving the rope and bedsheet to mine so there will be room for him to carry back the rations. *Don't forget this*, I say, handing him the tube of lip balm. He's the one whose lips can't handle the cold. As he zips up, Mama's voice fills my ears. *Don't split up.*

I push it aside and keep my eyes on D-39, who's snuffling around Papa's things like they're chew toys. I need something to focus on besides Papa and his leaving.

But Papa doesn't let me ignore him. He squeezes my arm. *I don't want to leave you, sugar girl. It's too risky. What if—*

He clamps his mouth shut, and I take a breath. I don't want him to leave me, either. But. *We need food*, I say. *And you'll be faster this way*. I grab D-39 around the neck. He's proof that I am not alone. I don't tell Papa what's really going on inside me, how my heart is so startlespooked I can feel it curling up on itself.

Even though it's what I want, and what I believe is right, all I can think is, *Mama left me, and now Papa is leaving me, too.* The only things we can give each other now are words.

Words

You'll come back? I say. *As soon as you're done?*

He nods. *Yes.*

You'll bring rations for D-39, too? Another nod, another yes. *You won't forget?*

I won't forget. He grabs my shoulders, and we wrap our arms around each other, upcuddling and squeezing.

Squeezing

Papa, how will I know it's you? When you come back? His brow furrows. *I'll knock. Okay? Like this.* He knocks on air: three short knocks, two long. *And you'll let me in.* I nod, even though my stomach squeezes with a python's grip.

Don't forget, he says. *You've got your screw-driver.* He taps a finger against my forehead. *And you've got all those hours taking things apart and putting them together again.* His voice turns gruff. *Klynt, you know things. Important things. You have skills other people don't.* I nod, though I'm not so sure.

He strokes my cheek. *Bye*, he says, leaving off the "good." Because it isn't good at all. Papa leaving is the opposite of good.

Good

Jopa's burrow has a real poopflush with whirlswirl water, a stove with two eyes that flare red with the turn of a dial. The trash goes into a compactor that sucks it up and out, so the underground room doesn't stink.

D-39, my very own sphinx, sits solemnly beside me as we watch Jopa and wait for him to wake up.

Wake Up

D-39 whines when Jopa's fingers move, and I jump. *Jopa?* His eyes shift beneath his lids, so I know he can hear me. *Jopa, it's me, Klynt.* I keep a hand on D-39 and my eyes on Jopa's face, searching for any other sign he's returning to the world.

All is still.

Jopa, I try again. *It's K-K.* What I would give to hear him say that silly nickname right now! *I've got your ants, Jopa.* I hard-press his palm against the glass jar. *D-39 is here, too. We're right here.*

Right Here

It takes a few hours, but finally Jopa's eyes pop open. *Hey*, I say, and rub his arm. *It's okay.* The words come out automatically, not because I'm sure they're true. His eyes shutterbug once, twice. He tries to lift himself, but I ease him back.

You were sleeping. I shrug. *Because of the deathstretch.* As if that explains everything. He lets out a sigh so big and long it's as if none of this is real. Instead we've been reading a book together and just now reached a bittersweet end to the story.

The Story

The next few hours pass like a slow parade. Jopa wigglesquirms his fingers and toes, then shifts his body on the cot. It's like watching a calf being born—without all the slime.

He sleeps. He tries to talk, but the only words that come out are garbled and confused. All the while I am waiting for the happily-ever-after: Papa's knock or any sound resembling Tiev and Dr. Tannin. But there's nothing and no one.

No One

Since no one is there to tell me, *Stop, don't, you shouldn't*, I open all the cabinets. The one that once held Jopa's favorite chocolate nubs is empty.

Even though there's the poopflush and stove and real working lights, the shelves are nearly as bare as the ones in our burrow. Dr. Tannin and Tiev need food as badly as we do.

No matter how many times I turn it over in my head, I can't make sense of what Dr. Tannin did to Jopa. *Stupid*, I think. Stupid, stupid, stupid.

Stupid

This is stupid, I say, just to hear my own voice. D-39's tail swishswipes like he's grateful that someone finally stated the obvious. I think of Mama at Everlake, across the border in the Wilds. Where we should have gone months or even years ago.

So stupid.

I'm about to stretch out on the couch beside D-39 when something roars above us. I curl myself into a ball like they taught us in school, so so long ago. Jopa screams his first clear word. *Boomblast!*

Boomblast

We duck as the walls quiverquake and dirt-dust crumbles from the ceiling. Hey hi ho there. The cease-fire is over. Which means rations day is over. A whole twenty-four hours have come and gone.

The bad news: Papa isn't back. Dr. Tannin isn't back. Tiev isn't back. It's still only me and D-39 and Jopa in the burrow.

Are you there, Mama? Are you listening? We are under attack, we're nearly out of food. Yet, there's good news, too. Jopa is sitting up, moving. Body and mind, awake.

Awake

Is it the deathstretch? Jopa asks.

I nod. *Yes.* He smacks his lips and reaches a hand out. *My ants.* I place the jar beside him on the cot and his face instantly relaxes. He keeps a hand on the jar as he looks around the room. *D-39.* At the sound of his name, D-39's tail swishwipes the air like a flag in a blusterblow. *Where's Tiev?* His eyes turn bigsky and wet, and his fingers curl into the sheet like claws. *And your papa?*

I don't want to, but I have to tell him the the facts.

The Facts

I don't know, I say. I tell him how Papa, D-39, and I found him. I hardpress my lips, hoping his tears don't make *me* dripface. I clear my throat. *Today is rations day.* And then I remember. *I mean, yesterday was rations day.* Jopa's brow creases, and he rubs his eyes. *How long have we been down here?*

I wish we didn't need to have this conversation. But as much as I want to protect Jopa from the truth, I know that even at his young age, he senses things. He *knows*. I owe it to him to tell him the truth, because he's a human being, and every human deserves that. So, as the boomblasts fatrattle the burrow and my heart squeezes for Papa, I tell him everything I know.

I Know

I'm hungry. D-39 is hungry. Jopa will be hungry soon.

After hearing my story, Jopa's quirk is less gappy than it used to be. *Mother and Tiev*, he starts. *They're fighters*. He straightens his shoulders. *Like these ants. Like me.*

That's right. I pat his leg. *You, me, we're all fighters. We have to be.* I grab his hand. *They'll be back soon*, I say with conviction.

Because one thing about Papa: He does what he says he will do. And he said he would come back. Whatever his faults, my father is a man of his word. His promises are the opposite of empty.

Empty

Jopa doesn't dripface, but his eyes bigsky at every fatrattle and distant boomblast. He watches D-39 pace, whine.

I hunch on the edge of his cot, trying to think of anything to help us get through these empty hours. *Hey*, I say to D-39, who's got something in his mouth. The edges are gnawed off, and the paper is crumpled, but I recognize it right away. My heart hollows out. It's Papa's map of the Worselands and the Wilds. It's got all the roads and humpbacks and valleys. I'm sure Papa didn't mean to leave it behind. This map should be in his pack.

D-39, I sweetmurmur. *Where'd you get this?* My robo probably found it behind the couch. It must have fallen when Papa was rearranging his pack. Or worse, D-39 snagged it when neither of us was looking.

I don't like thinking about Papa out there without a map. Is that why he's not back yet? Is he lost? There are so many possible reasons for his delay.

Delay

I can't think about Papa. Surely he knows the way without a map. To distract myself I grab the book from my pack. *Want me to read to you?* I don't wait for an answer. I simply open the cover, turn to the start of chapter one, and without delay, begin reading to Jopa.

Reading to Jopa

The only book we brought with us from our burrow is called *The Giver*. Because we'd only just started it, and I convinced Papa that we could always use the pages for kindling when we finished it.

The book's about a boy named Jonas who gets a different assignment from the one he was expecting. Already I can tell Jonas is a hero because he thinks for himself. He has his own opinions and makes his own choices.

I keep reading even after Jopa's eyes close. I wish Papa were here so I could ask him if he chose a survival book on purpose. Also, I'd like to know: What's *my* assignment?

Assignment

I can't sleep no matter how much my eyes ache. All that time in the burrow I thought I would be happier without Papa, and now I want to hear his snore, see him whittling. His voice echoes in my mind: *Wait*. Then Mama's voice, louder than ever: *Everlake, Everlake, Everlake*. I curl myself around D-39 and let my eyes fall on Jopa, who's sleeping peacefully. Is he my assignment? I press my hands over my ears and pray for food, for Papa, for the deathstretch to reach its end.

End

I finish the book about Jonas right before Jopa wakes. I read the last page for a second time aloud to D-39, and then for a third time to Jopa. Jonas saves the baby, and after everything, they sled down a hill toward a cabin with lights—they don't die.

At least I don't think they do. Jopa says he's not so sure, but he wasn't exactly awake for the whole book. I'm thinking about it when I stir water into a bowl of instant loogameal. Sometimes what we think is the end isn't the end at all. *Hungry?* I ask Jopa and hand him the spoon. *Take it slow.*

Slow

It takes a while, but soon Jopa's muscles remember how to feed, how to stand, how to walk. He's slow because his body is weak from so much medicated sleeping. Good thing he watched Tiev doing all that exercising. He understands that's what it takes to get strong, his sister's kind of dedication, and it's not going to happen in just a day or two. It's a process. I don't know what else to do, so on the third day without Papa I pretend I'm Jopa's teacher and the burrow is a classroom.

Classroom

Let's reinvent the ticktock, I say. Mostly because I know it will make me feel better—more in control—if I tinker. Plus I can't stand the numbers. The glacial *tick tick tick* sounds so much like the knock that never comes. But there is nothing to be done without screws, gears, or other parts, so Jopa and I cut pie pieces out of colored paper like in kinderschool—except no plastic scissors.

I use my screwdriver to poke holes, then Jopa folds and tears as D-39 watches intently. When Jopa pulls a bottle of glue from the bin marked *art supplies*, I shake my head. Art supplies in a burrow. Dr. Tannin thought of things we didn't. If Mama still lived with us, would we have had art supplies in our burrow, too?

When we're finished, there are no more digits. Seven pie pieces labeled *EAT, SLEEP, SPARKSHINE, READ, SURVIVAL TRAINING, FITNESS*, and *REMEMBER*. I hand the ticktock to Jopa. *Pick one—your choice.*

Choice

Survival Training, he says. *Okay*, I say, mentally scanning the things I've learned. I start with the first thing Papa told me when we were stocking the burrow. *Listen to what your body tells you.*

Jopa cocks his head like D-39 does when he encounters something new. So I try to explain about that feeling in the pit of your stomach or when the hair on the back of your neck prickletwitches. The intuition or instinct that wild animals seem to trust without question. But we humans choose whether to pay attention or not. *Your body knows before you do. You can save your own life if you listen. Got it?*

He nods. *So you're saying to be like an ant. Don't get squashed.* I snickergiggle. *Can ants hear? Do they even have ears?*

Nope, Jopa says. *They hear by feeling vibrations through the ground with their feet.* I ruffle his hair, then reach into my back pocket. Kid's going to be an entomologist one day, I just know it. If we can survive this. *Okay.* I press my lips together. *Now. Do you know how to use a slingshot?*

Slingshot

We practice by loading it with Lego pieces because that's all we can find. *Stones are heavier,* I tell Jopa so he knows it will be different in the wild.

This is fun, Jopa says. We practice aiming and shooting for nearly an hour. D-39 watches for a while, then settles into sleep-mode. Soon Jopa gets tired, too, so I return the slingshot to my pocket. I let my breath out, joyslammed for the respite from the boomblasts. *Now let's do REMEMBER.*

Remember

Jopa and I both sit on the floor in the main room, our backs to the small sofa. I wish I could remember what the world was like before BrkX, when Mama was my mother, and there was no K-9 Corridor. I wish we were back in the world of type-writers and printing presses. I wish Jopa and I had stories to share about real dogs, like Sounder and Lassie. But that's not the world we live in. And as much as I don't want to, we have to talk more about what's happened to us, about what happened before Papa and I left our burrow. We must discuss the skysail and the big boomblast that landed us here.

Here

I call D-39 to my side, and he settles next to my leg. *Okay, Jopa, tell me what you remember about the day the big boomblast came.* He takes a noisy breath. *The skysail. It flew so high!* He wrinkles his nose. *Tiev was flipfurious. She said it was my fault.*

I shake my head. *It wasn't your fault. It was mine.* Jopa leans his head against the couch, his face reddening as the words hurryscurry out. *While the boomblasts kept coming, we were waiting for Mother to get back from her shift at the clinic, only she didn't come and she didn't come.* He takes a quick breath. *Tiev told me to stay put while she went out to check the clinic.* I lean toward him, a little breathless. *Wait*, I say. *She left you? Alone?*

It was fine, he says. *She gave me a bunch of chocolate nubs to eat while she was away.* He quirkfaces. *She was only gone a few hours.*

Chocolate nubs. The kid will do anything for candy. *Where did she go? Did she find your mom?* Jopa nods. *She said Mother was busy at the clinic, and Mother told her we better not leave the burrow again. Then Tiev gave me a fizzy drink. The next thing I remember is you when I woke up.*

My heart buckles. *You mean it's just been you and Tiev the whole time? I thought—* I don't know what I thought. Probably better to stick to Jopa's story, though. I don't want to alarm him before I've had a chance to gather all the information. *So Tiev was the one who put you to sleep.* Jopa shrugs. *I guess.*

Guess

I clamp my jaw shut. I know what that means—something happened to keep Dr. Tannin from coming back to the burrow. But I don't know what. Jopa stares at me with his bigsky eyes. *What?*

I don't want to hypothesize in front of Jopa. I don't want to say anything more about his mother, about what might have happened to her. Besides, it's better to be optimistic. It's just as likely that Dr. Tannin is fine as it is that she's not. Just because she didn't make it back to the burrow doesn't mean she's dead. She could be at the clinic still or stuck in some other burrow. Who knows? May as well believe in the good thing instead of the bad.

I can't help stiffening when I think of Tiev putting Jopa under. How convenient—how much easier for her to complete her endless workouts if Jopa was sleeping? I shake my head to clear the thought. I'm fine, D-39 is fine, Jopa is fine. No sense speculating about who did what and why or who's alive and who's dead.

Dead

My heartbeat fills my ears as I pull back the paper on the ticktock and see that the hands have stopped moving. The battery must be dead. Surely it's nearly bedtime again, and still Papa hasn't returned. I rub the back of my neck. Three days. Papa should have been back a long time ago. We eat the last can of baga stew. We read, and then Jopa picks *FITNESS*. He says, *So I can surprise Tiev.* Together we do a full burrow workout.

Burrow Workout

Meatscramble can in one hand, jar of panchobeans in the other. Lift, lift, lift. High-knees. Up-downs. D-39 beside us like we are a football team of three. A hundred crunches, fifty push-ups. Run, run, run in place. *You're getting strong*, I tell Jopa. He flexes his muscles. *I'm already strong.* I chuckle, correct myself. *StrongER.* He lifts his arms like a boxer who just won a huge fight. *StrongEST.*

Strongest

I make Jopa brush his teeth even though he wants to go straight to sleep. I read to him even though I'm so worried about Papa and Tiev and Dr. Tannin that I can't concentrate on the story, I can only say the words. *Let's sing,* Jopa says, when I try to tuck him in. *Sing what?* I say. He giggles. *Anything.*

So we sing. About ants. *Worker ants feed and clean, feed and clean, feed and clean all morning.* Not once does Jopa fuss at me to go faster or say I'm off key or tell me the words are wrong—even though they probably are. *Soldier ants fight and guard, fight and guard, fight and guard all morning.* Even D-39 joins in with a howl at the very end, and Jopa says it's the best chorus ever.

When Jopa closes his eyes and we say good night, I make him a silent promise: Whatever happens during the rest of the deathstretch, there will be no medication for us. No fizzy drinks, no needles pushing fluid into our veins. We'll stay awake for everything. Even the bad stuff. No matter what, we'll stick together. Jopa, D-39, and me. We're strongest that way, side by side by side.

Side by Side

I lie awake with D-39 for a long time, my eyelids still shutterbugging long after his have dropped shut. A memory comes to me of Papa making sugar toast. He'd heat butter and sugar in a skillet, drop two pieces of wheatkins in—one for him, one for me—and swirl and swirl them like he was making a painting.

I miss his pipe and his scruffy face and his scowl. His last words echo in my ears: *Klynt, you know things.* I'm listening to my body—my stomach and head and neck—and they all say the same thing. Something is jayballs wrong, or he would be here.

As fancy as this burrow is, we're nearly out of food. Jopa and I can't keep waiting. If I were a hero in a book, we wouldn't wait at all. Jonas didn't wait in *The Giver*. The time has come for me to decide the next step.

Next Step

I can't sleep, so I ease away from D-39. He lifts his head to watch me, but when I whisper, *It's okay*, he settles back into sleepmode. Jopa rolls over, but he doesn't wake. I shuffle through Papa's things until I find the dogchewed map. I locate the International Peace Garden, which is on the border, and I run my finger across our town, which is south and west of the garden, maybe thirty-five miles. I squint-check and draw my finger north and east.

That's when I see it: Everlake. It's right in the same close-but-so-far-away place it's always been. No roads from here to there— just rows of humpbacks. Humpbacks that hide buttes, valleys, and lakes, all untamed and wild. Mama's Everlake, hidden. But here on this map, it blazes with a faint, penciled-in star.

Star

When Jopa wakes on what I think is the fourth day without Papa, I tell him what we must do. *Something's happened. It's been too long. We've got to go where there's food, where it's safe.* I tell him about Mama and about Everlake. *It's not that far*, I say. *Just across the border.*

The distance between here and that tiny star looks like nothing on the map, but I know it's not that easy. There's a death-stretch going on, for one. The border with its towers, wires, walls, robopatrols. And to make it even more challenging, all those humpbacks will require lots of up and down and walking around. It won't be a straight shot. We're likely to encounter all sorts of wildlife, some of it dangerous—bears, moose, badgers.

I quiverquake. And the cherry on top: Let's not forget the weather. Freezeseason in these parts kills people and animals every single year. Keeping ourselves warm and dry will be a top priority. For D-39, too. Who knows what freezing temps and cold-dust will do to a robo? But I don't mention these concerns to Jopa because I don't want to startlespook him.

His eyes get shiny, but he doesn't dripface. *Mother and Tiev will be flipfurious if they come back and I'm not here.* I grab his hand. *No,* I say. *Not flipfurious. They'll be joyslammed, because it will mean you're okay. They'll know you got out.* His voice turns itchtwitchy. *But shouldn't we wait for them? Isn't that what they wanted?* I throw an arm around his shoulder and pull him toward me. *I don't know what they wanted. Except I know this.* I make him meet my eyes. *You mean more to them than anything. They want you to be alive and safe.* Even if they're not.

Not

I ramscramble for some words that will convince Jopa. I need him strong and determined to be that fighter again. Not upset. *Listen, they could be anywhere. And it's most dangerous here in the deathstretch zone. Our best bet is to go. To Everlake. And then we'll come back when the deathstretch is over.*

He studies me. *Can I bring my ants?* I nod. *Of course.* When I show him how we can nestle the jar in the pack, his fists unclench. *We'll come back? After the death-stretch? To find them?*

I grab his hand. *Of course we will. Of course. And there are dogs there, Jopa! Not just robos. Real dogs. We'll get to pet them, and we'll have a whole adventure to tell both our families. They'll be proud of us. You'll see.*

D-39 whines like he knows I'm not exactly telling the truth. Like he knows that what's tumbling out of my mouth may be shaped like words, but what I'm selling is actually hope.

Hope

Instead of making me want to take the words back, D-39's whine fills me with an urgency and faith in this new plan. I want to do whatever I can to make the words I'm saying to Jopa actually turn out to be true. *We'll come back, I promise. And Papa will know where we are. I know he will. And he'll tell your mom and Tiev.* His whole face lights up as the names of his loved ones fill the burrow. I lean my head against D-39's shoulder and take a big breath. Please, let these words I'm saying turn out to be genuine!

Genuine

As I pack and repack the rope and map and bedsheet, boomblasts fatrattle the dishes. D-39 paces, whines. Jopa pulls a grocery sack from beneath the sofa. *To wrap my ant jar in*, he says. *In case it breaks.*

I fuel up D-39, using the last drops from the can, and pray it will be enough to get us there. As Jopa and I share the last jar of panchobeans, I'm filled with doubt: What if I forget something important? What if we get lost? What if I don't remember how to tie a bowline, make a fire, fillet a fish?

What if we get caught by soldiers? What if Jopa is too weak or D-39 runs off or Papa comes back right after we've gone? I drop my head into my hands, and my hair flops into my face. *I'm sorry we have to do this, Jopa.* I mean it in the sincerest way possible. Because I am sorry. I really am. *But we've got no choice.*

What I mean is, we can't sit here and do nothing. This—this exactly—is what Papa trained me for. It has to be the right thing to do. Doesn't it? *If we want to eat*, I tell Jopa in my most confident voice, *if we want to find our families, our best chance is out there.*

Out There

As D-39 paces and whines, I climb the stairs and turn the crank that opens the hatch. Jopa stays at the bottom of the steps with D-39. I'm so focused on my task that at first I don't hear the tapping. It's D-39's sharp bark that alerts me.

Then I do hear it, and so does Jopa. *Someone's knocking,* he says before his face droopbottoms. *Not Mother or Tiev, because they wouldn't knock.* My eyes bigsky. *Could it be Papa?* It's not the knock that we discussed, but Papa could be injured or weak from dehydration.

I turn the crank faster. To think he's back as we're about to leave! My breath whifflegusts as I push the hatch open.

Open

Brisk air blasts my face, and the first
thing I see is the barrel of a gun. Boots.
Pants so dingy I can't tell what color they
started out.

I grab the stair railing and shout at Jopa,
Get back! Someone—living and breathing
and stinking—pushes in.

Not a robofighter, thank goodness. A man.

Man

I thrust out my chest and pull my shoulders back to make myself tall, even though I want to be anywhere but here. The man's face is smudged, his hair like a lion's mane. He smells of a mix of sewage and exhaust—like he hasn't bathed in years. His clothes hang off his thin shoulders. His eyes are red-rimmed and hungry.

He points the gun at us. *Anyone else here?* His voice reminds me of a movie villain. I want to lie, to tell him our parents are waiting behind the curtain, but he doesn't pause for an answer. He swings past us, makes a brisk search of the place. *Just what I need*, he says. *Two kids and a robo.* The man relaxes his gun, and it's like my brain is caught in some twilight zone. Is this man good or bad?

Who are you? Jopa says. The man stares at us, then lets out a cackle so menacing that even wolves would run from it. D-39's lip curls back, and he growls low in his throat, in attack mode. *We were just leaving*, I announce, and I quick pull my robo and Jopa upstairs.

Upstairs

I don't stop to look before I pop my head out of the opening. The thin blue metal truck bed is bent back, so it no longer hides the hatch. I wonder if the lion-man did that, or someone—or something—else did.

D-39 scrambles out ahead of me, all quirk-face and plumy tail. The hatch and burrow and lion-man are no match for the bigsky world with its many sights and scents.

Jopa moves in slow-mo, like he did when he first awoke from the medication, not at all like the can't-stop-him boy I used to know. I help pull him up and out, and as soon as his feet clear the opening, the lion-man's hard-edged voice rises from the burrow. *Wait!* he says. *You won't last the night!* As if he's concerned about us.

But my animal body thrums with alarm. It's too risky. We don't know this man, and we were leaving anyway. I push the hatch, and my heart quiverquakes as it bangs down behind us.

V.

Behind Us

The sky hangs dirty-dishwater gray, and a blusterblow ruffles the remains of Jopa's house beside the broken-down blue truck. I crouch beside Jopa, half waiting for the lion-man to burst out of the hatch. When he doesn't, my breathing begins to slow. My eyes follow D-39, who strides away, sniffs something, circles, and comes back to check on us. Everything's okay. We're okay.

Wow, Jopa says, and I remember this is his first time seeing the world since the big boomblast. I give him a jinglesnap to take it all in. I was so sure leaving the burrow was the right thing, but now I don't know. And it's too late to change my mind, because the lion-man's in there.

I focus on my breathing. *In. Out. In. Out.* In only a handful of days it's turned to freeze-season. No wonder the lion-man was so eager to invade our burrow.

I scan from our safe spot behind the blue sheet of metal. Where are you, Papa? There are no more people, no men or soldiers or anyone. At least not that I can see.

But we can't stay here. Not when the lion-man and his gun could pop out at any moment. *What now?* Jopa says, his hands gripping the ant jar in its bag. He looks at me like I know what I'm doing, like I really am a leader or hero. I don't want to disappoint him, so I grab his hand. We leave the house behind us. *Run!*

Run

We stumble forward, when what I want to do is fly. D-39 darts ahead, doubles back, leaps over a three-legged chair. When he reaches me, he licks my hand with his slipsloppy tongue as if to say, *Faster!*

My heart thudjams, my skin tingles with cold, and my toes prickletwitch. I'm so ready to go. But I can feel Jopa's shoulders quiverquaking from fear or cold—I'm not sure which. *Hey*, I say, and slow our pace as we pass another pile of rubbish. *We need coats. Blankets.*

Lots of them, Jopa says, his teeth clacking. And not just blankets, I think, but don't say. We need the sky to hold off on snow. We need to travel light and fast, with no mishaps. We need high-energy food, ample water, and a million other things to make it safely to our destination. Jopa won't get very far without rest and recovery time. But how can we stop, when we don't know what or who is out there? As we scour the remains around us, I hold my screwdriver in attack position, determined to keep all three of us safe and warm.

Warm

Jopa's whole body shuddershakes, and he hunches like an old man. I think it's because of how long he slept. Even after the time with me in the burrow, he's still not totally normal.

I follow D-39 as he noses around. He's like a detective-robo. When he finds a knit afghan, he snuffles, sneezes. *Good boy*, I say and drape it over Jopa's shoulders, even though it could cover him double.

He quirkfaces. *Super Jopa!* He stretches his arms and pretends to be a redhawk that swoops for prey. It's such a normal Jopa thing to do, I snickergiggle.

I shrug into a wool coat that looks like it could fit Papa. When I dip my hands into the pockets, I find gloves. *Look, Jopa! We can take turns wearing them.* I slip them onto Jopa's hands right away.

Right Away

With the gloves on, Jopa stands a little straighter. D-39 sidles up to investigate. *Good robo*, Jopa says, reaching to pet him. Quick as anything, D-39 right away snags a glove in his teeth, yanks it off Jopa's hand, and saunters forward.

Jopa yelps, and D-39 looks back at us, quirkfacing. The prize dangles from his mouth like it's the best trick ever. We snickergiggle, and for a jinglesnap I forget about the deathstretch, the rubble, Papa not coming back. I forget about Jopa's weakness. I'm ready for anything.

Anything

Anything can happen during a deathstretch, Jopa says, once I recover the glove from D-39's teeth. His words come out smoother now that he's warmer. *That's what Mother says.*

Your mother's a smart lady, I say. The grave uncertainty of our situation is not what I want to think about when we're exposed like this, with boomblasts snapcrackling in the distance.

We've got to keep moving. Like I know where we're going. But the three of us weave our way onto what was once the road.

The Road

Empty yet full of garbage. Like we're the only people in our town, in the Worselands, in the whole bigsky world. I want to call out, *Papa!*

He must be close. He *must* be. But there might be another lion-man on the road or a robopatrol or worse.

Worse

We walk until the sky turns dark. Not black like in the burrow, not the shadowy black backlit by distant fires, or black cut by streaking boomblasts.

Instead, gray-black. Just enough light to see how alone we are, how small. It's creepy in a what-will-happen-next kind of way, and goose bumps rise on my arms.

I can't believe a desperado claimed our burrow, Jopa says. *Mother's not going to like that.* I lift the pack with my arms to ease the pressure of the straps digging into my shoulders. I can't believe it either. Sure, we were leaving, but what if we hadn't been? What if we'd been forced out without any supplies? He had a gun—the lion-man easily could've killed us.

I suck in my breath. What will happen when Papa or Dr. Tannin and Tiev come back? They won't know it's not us in there. They'll walk into a trap! Which is way worse than what happened to us.

I shake my head. So stupid! Why didn't I leave some sign? Some sort of signal? Something to let them know to be careful? Because I'm still not sure if the lion-man was just scary looking or if he really meant to hurt us.

As D-39 skirts around another pile of rubble and we follow, I pray out loud for the first time in my life: *Please, God, let Papa and the others be okay when they come back. And please, please, please let us walk in the correct direction.*

Direction

When Jopa stumbles to his knees for the fifteenth time, I know we have to stop. But where?

Think like an animal, I remind myself. Wolf or bear or deer or rabbit. Because animals use all the clues around them to determine the best direction.

So I pretend. I creepcrawl along, quiet and watchful, just like D-39.

Warmth, my animal-self thinks. Hydration. Camouflage. Rest.

Rest

We settle beneath a strip of metal roofing that's been ripclawed from somewhere—a barn, maybe. Now it's bent and propped on a mound of rubble like a cone-shaped party hat. Not much cover, but enough.

I climb in first to make a little nest for Jopa. As he settles in, I tuck the afghan around him. D-39 stretches along his side, as if taking advantage of the warmth. Either he was programmed for closeness, or he's learned it during his time with me.

Jopa throws an arm around D-39 and closes his eyes. I settle in on the other side of D-39, even though my stomach is grumbly and it's hard to think of anything except water. But that will have to wait until morning.

Soon D-39's hummingbird-quiet motor cuts off, and he emits the faintest drone that tells me he's in sleepmode. That's when I know that I, too, can close my eyes and dream of a new day.

New Day

Frosty. Inside the party hat my breath is visible, and my ears and nose are numb. I rise slowly and poke my head out, my mind adjusting again to the real world: black ruins, no cover except for this wreckage.

As the first sunrays peek over the piles of debris, my stomach is as hollow as a bird-house with no bird. My throat is as dry and crackly as a prairie fire.

Jopa stretches, almost quirkfaces. *It's the morning?* he asks, and I nod. D-39's eyes shutterbug open, dark and warm. His chestplate shows no sign of red rings. My shoulders loosen as he stretches, and I rub his belly. In spite of everything, here we are. As he heads out to do his business— plumy tail swishswiping like always—I pull out the map.

Map

According to the position of the sun, I know we are heading north, like we should be. *How can you tell?* Jopa wants to know. So I explain about compasses and how the sun rises in the east and sets in the west. I show him on the map what looks like the thin tine of a comb. It's actually the river we will follow for a while. It helps divert our minds away from hunger and thirst as we clamber over and duck between artifacts: a cracked poopflush, a door, a flowerpot. Farmhouses in pieces and scattered like dandelion puffs.

I can't help but scan for items to add to my museum until I remember there is no more museum. *Look at that!* Jopa says when D-39 comes back to us carrying an unopened pack of sweet cinnamon crunchballs. Jopa opens the package, and I divide them into three—a palmful for each of us. It isn't much, but it helps us keep moving. Oh so slowly, we pick our way to the place where the hidden trickling creek ends, bigskying into a river.

River

Before: A wide green ribbon. Shallow, rocky, all gentle gurgle and croon—except after a storm when it would rush and roar and froth. A home for frogs and slender, darting fish. Where crayfish made their muddy tunnels. Its banks sheltered by swaying tallgrass urging, singing, *Sit and stay.*

Sit and Stay

Now: The water runs rusty, and the river's banks are barricaded by strewn lumber. An upside-down table, two legs jutting in the air, the others splintered. A half-shattered lamp. Instead of song, barely a murmur. Flies swarm, humming loud enough to rival Papa's chug-chug. And the odor of decaying bodies—so much worse than the lion-man. Black as death.

Don't look, I tell Jopa, but he does anyway. I cringe when he gasps. Even though I command D-39 to *sit, stay,* my robo leaps into the water before I can stop him.

Stop Him

D-39 stands hip-deep and starts drinking. His tongue lap, lap, lapping. *No, D-39!* I grab his collar and yank him away. *That's nasty.* Jopa pulls the afghan tighter around himself. *Can't hurt a robo, can it?* I shrug because I'm not sure. *I forget sometimes that he's a robo*, I confess. Either way, I don't want D-39 getting familiar with the smell of death.

I'm so thirsty, Jopa whines. *Me too*, I tell him. My tongue positively aches from thirst. But Papa warned about unfiltered water and how it can make a person so sick they can't move. It could even kill us. *Give me a minute.* I pull the filter from my pack and operate it the way Papa taught me. We sit on the ground crisscross applesauce, so a spill is less likely. I drop one end of the tube into the river, then ask Jopa to hold the other end over the cup. I pump and pump, but we only get a trickle at a time. The water moves so slowly that I worry we will thirst to death before the water is clean enough to drink.

To Drink

How much longer? Jopa asks, his voice
raspy. *Almost there*, I tell him. *Hey*, I say.
Let's talk about ants. Jopa right away starts
listing off species: *carpenter, harvester,
weaver, fire.* I bet ants everywhere would
be joyslammed to know that they have
such power of distraction.

Finally the water is ready—one cup shared
by all of us. I offer it to Jopa. *You first.* I
count the swallows out loud to help him go
slowly and savor it. *One, two, three.* Next
it's my turn. I take tiny flutterbug sips,
because it's hard to drink anything while
sitting next to the rancid river. When I
set the cup on the ground in front of D-39,
he sniffs it, but doesn't drink. I scratch
behind his ears. *Go ahead. It's for you.* But
he settles onto the bank, head in his paws.
I turn to Jopa. *You take it.* This time he
swallows it in one long swig, no counting.
I pray for freshwash because this filtering
takes entirely too long. Now all we need is
something to eat.

Something to Eat

My screwdriver is sharp, ready. That last
jar of panchobeans seems ages ago even
though it was yesterday. I turn to Jopa.
Got the slingshot? He shows me a palmful of
small stones. *Will these do?*

I load a stone. *One way to find out.* What
we need is a rabbit or squirrel. Something
small, but not too small. As he watches us,
D-39's ears twitch like weather vanes, the
way they do when he's hunting.

Hunting

While we stake out a spot behind a big boulder, I gather four sticks, like Papa taught me. I pull a piece of rope from my pack and bind them together, so it looks like a four-pronged fork. *Superfork*, I say proudly, and Jopa quirkfaces. *Super K-K*. I roll my shoulders back. It's silly, but somehow it makes me feel powerful. I crouch, weapon in hand, waiting for prey.

A yellowlark calls. Another answers. *Good*, I sweetmurmur. D-39 lifts his head, like he knows exactly what I'm thinking. I hand Jopa the slingshot so he can be the one to fire the first stone.

The First Stone

Branch snaps, wings whirr—no bird. Jopa
loads again, shoots again. Misses. Misses.
Keeps on missing.

Missing

Jopa frowns, and it makes me think of
Papa. His humpgrump mouth and the way
his face transforms when he smokes his
pipe. How when Mama left, he stayed. He
stayed with me. Mama got to be the hero,
and he stayed.

How Papa took me to the pit to trade D-39
and let me bring him home instead. How
his eyes light when he talks about the
looganuts. The gentleness of his bigsky,
sunburned hands spreading loogabutter
across wheatkins. All the ways he cares
for me that I never really pay attention
to—until today. I want so much to tell him
that I see it now. I get it. I get *him*. But he's
not here.

Not Here

I shake away my droopbottom thoughts and focus on Everlake. *Wait till you see it*, I tell Jopa as we stalk another yellowlark. He likes the way the name twinkles. When I tell him about dancers on skates slicing ice and dogs fetching flydiscs, his eyes glimmerspark. *D-39's going to love it*, he says. I check in with my robo, calling his name softly. Right away D-39 meets my gaze as if to say, *I'm listening. What do you need me to do?* I don't tell Jopa that everything is only in my imagination. I've never been there. *It's going to be great*, I say. *Mother and Tiev will like it, too*, Jopa says. *Yes*, I say. *I think they will.* Who wouldn't love a place with so much freedom after living in the Worselands?

Oh, how I wish for the ham radio! I'd like to send out a message to Jopa's family. Something like, *Hey hi ho there. If you're out there, Dr. Tannin and Tiev, Jopa will be waiting for you at Everlake.* If we can ever get there.

Get There

I miss them, Jopa says. When I notice his lip quiverquaking, I throw my arm around his shoulder. *I know you do. You're being so, so brave, Jopa. They're going to be proud of you!* I want to say something to keep Jopa going so he doesn't collapse into tears and slow us down even more. Something to keep us both going.

At Everlake I bet there's whole new species of ants. We just have to get there. *Who knows what kind you might discover?* His eyes, still wet, bigsky. *Subterranean ants? The ones that look like emeralds?* I shrug. *Maybe.* He pumps his fist. *Yes.*

Jopa tells me more about the emerald-colored ants as we walk, how they spend their lives underground. I can't help remembering what it was like in the burrow, when all I wanted in that dark, smelly hole was to see the sky.

And now here we are, beneath beautiful blue canopy, and all I want now is for it to end, for this journey to be over.

Over

We're just about to target another bird for lunch when the first drop hits me on the top of my left ear. It's cold. I look up, and almost-frozen-but-not-quite freshwash drops needle my face. The drought is over. I stick out my tongue to catch a few drops, grateful for any excuse to stop walking. D-39 makes a circle as misty droplets cling to his faux fur. The air smells fresh, like greenseason, not at all like the beginning of freezeseason. As the moisture sinks into my shoes, my toes alternate between achy and numb. It's so distracting, the freshwash has been coming down for a good five minutes before I realize this is our chance.

Chance

Help me, I say to Jopa. *We need to catch as much freshwash as we can.* He pockets the slingshot and carefully unwraps his jar of ants. *We can use the bag*, he says and stretches the plastic grocery sack open so it can collect the drizzly downpour. *Great idea*, I tell Jopa, and it is. But something more sturdy would be even better. D-39 follows as I thread through remains and right a poopflush. It's kind of disgusting to think about, but if we could plug it, it might make a good bowl. Worth taking a chance. I tidywipe it, block the opening with my T-shirt. Right away it begins to fill. Jopa and I drink from cupped hands as freshwash continues to fall. Still, D-39 refuses. By the time the clouds move off and the sky lightens, I can no longer ignore the way my shoulders and arms and legs have turned stiff as concrete.

Concrete

The wet-cold prickletwitches my skin, and
my stomach fistclenches as I realize the
next time this happens it's likely to be
cold-dust burying the road and turning us
to popsicles. We don't have much time to
get to Everlake safely, and it's still probably
twenty miles away. *Come on*, I say to Jopa.
We retreat to a patch of concrete beside a
half-collapsed grain elevator where it isn't
dry but drier. *What about lunch?* he asks,
but I ignore him. I press the damp map
deeper inside my shirt and scoop as much
freshwash as I can from the poopflush into
Jopa's grocery sack, which is what passes
as a canteen. I hear Mama's voice: *Hurry*.

Hurry

When the sun comes back out, so do the animals. The land comes alive with chirps, whistles, and yellowlark song. Finally we see the small game we've been hoping for. Lizards scurry, mice scamper, squirrels forage for nuts. A rabbit twitches its nose, hop-hops to nibble a little, then stops to twitch some more. I motion to Jopa to hold on to D-39's collar, and once my robo's secure, I lift the superfork from my pack. My arm prickletwitches as I squintcheck, testing my aim. The rabbit is still there, but I've got to hurry. I close my eyes and press the superfork downdown into the rabbit's back. The rabbit squeals—all pain and fury. I almost can't stand it, so I use my screwdriver like a knife, stab the rabbit quick and don't look again until it stops struggling.

Struggling

When I hold the dead rabbit, still warm, in my hands, I want to lift it triumphantly, like the time I finished my first row of dropping and covering looganut seeds without Papa correcting or complaining. And I also want to dripface. It's like my emotions are constantly struggling with one another, and I am never sure which one will win out.

D-39 sniffs and jerkwags his tail, eyes never leaving the rabbit. He is confident, sure in all the ways I want to be. Jopa's eyes glimmerspark with hunger. *Do you know how to build a fire?* he asks. I nod because thanks to Papa, I *do* know how to build a fire.

How to Build a Fire

Bundle a ball of birdnest fluff or cotton balls for the middle. Smear it with lip balm. Gather wood in three sizes: thick, like your arm, sticks like pencils, and toothpick-thin twigs. Arrange wood pieces vertically around the bundled-up ball in the middle, leaving plenty of space for air. Which sounds great, except all of that is impossible when the world is wet.

Wet

Any wood we find is freshwash-soaked, and we are, too. If only we could shake it off, like D-39 does. My fingers are stiff with cold, and I've got no cache of sticks, no cotton balls, no lip balm.

No lighter, no matches, no batteries to throw a spark, even if the logs were dry. *I can't do rabbit sushi*, I tell Jopa. *Can we keep it?* he asks. *Carry it with us for later?* I don't answer right away because it's not a bad idea. Except D-39 is doing his sphinx thing, watching the rabbit. *Why don't we give this one to D-39?* I say. Jopa agrees, so I toss the rabbit to D-39, who grabs it gently in his teeth and carries it behind a fallen leafgiant like he knows we can't bear to watch him eat.

Eat

Jopa and I forage nearby piles of rubble for anything edible—nuts, berries—while my stomach growls for potato crisps. Crunchy, salty, finger-licking greasy.

How long since I've tasted potato crisps? A year? Two? When we come to a fallen cressnut leafgiant with fat nuts on branches and nutshells littering the ground, I know the fruit is still good—if the squirrels haven't already stockpiled it all. I scour the place. Find one nut, two, a dozen.

Jopa's small hands can't hold many nuts, and he doesn't know how to shell them without a nutcracker tool. Lucky for us both, Papa taught me a cressnut trick. So while D-39 dozes beside us, I put two nuts in my hand, one's ridge against another's indention and squeeze. Pick out the meat for Jopa.

For Jopa

After the cressnuts, I scrounge around and find what looks like a kitchen drawer, its contents half-buried in mud. I make up a story about who it belonged to: an old couple who thought they'd seen it all. *And now*, I tell Jopa, *they're right below us*. I tap the ground with my foot.

Jopa's face pales, and I realize he's misunderstood me. *Not dead*, I say. *They're all snug in a burrow, playing a card game or something*. I dig around some more until I spy a piece of rainbow fabric. At first I think it can't be what I think it is. We've walked ten miles today, maybe more. My heart rammerjammers as I pull it up and out. I can't believe it, but it *is* what I think it is. It really is.

Look, I call to Jopa and lift up the rainbow skysail with a duct-taped T-shaped patch, its string in a wad, all snarled and gray. Jopa shrieks. *Our skysail!* He upcuddles it and fingers the string, gently easing the tangle like it's a string of rare, precious pearls. *Thank you*, he singsongs, and for the first time all day I quirkface. I wonder: Was finding the skysail a miracle or fate?

Fate

We charge ahead, sore feet and wet-cold clothing forgotten for the moment. I expect D-39 to leap up like he normally does, but he stays on the ground. *D-39*, I call. *Come*. But he doesn't come. When I crouch beside him, he lifts his head in slow-mo, and his eyelids droop. I rub him behind his scratchpatched ear. *Was the rabbit that good? Now you gotta take a nap?* His tail swishswipes but only slightly, and I realize my robo is failing. I check his m-fuel level, and it's fine for now. *You're okay, D-39*, I soothe, even though I'm not sure he is.

You don't have to be a restoration expert to know that no robo was designed for this kind of exposure. It's lucky he's operated so long and so well. But this can't be his fate—not before we get to Everlake. I examine his chestplate. *Can you fix him?* Jopa asks, huddling beside us to get a look for himself. *Hopefully there's a setting or something I can adjust*. I haven't even gotten my screwdriver all the way out when the hair on the back of my neck lifts, prickletwitches in the way that means watch out.

Watch Out

I rest my hand on D-39's head as I scan the rolling prairie. I take in the white-faced buttes, the rusting metal arm of an ancient abandoned oil well. It feels like we're being watched. Maybe it's a coyote or wolf.

Then I see it: a plume of smoke rising and tapering, a deepdark scarf trailing the sky's neck. And I know it's not a coyote, not a wolf.

Not a Wolf

I grab Jopa's arm, point to the smoke.
Shhhhh. Could be a hungry, homeless outlaw
like the lion-man back at Jopa's burrow.
A soldier, maybe, or a troop of them. An
armed robofighter. Or something else.

Something Else

It could also be ordinary people like us. Regular people trying to survive the deathstretch. A family who would welcome us, maybe even help us.

I want to believe that, to meet these imaginary people and bathe in the warmth of smoke and fire, and I want something else, like information about where we are and what's happening with the deathstretch. Maybe tell them about Papa and ask, *Have you seen Link Tovis?* My stomach tells me it's best to stay quiet.

But Jopa's stomach must tell him something else, because he waves his arms in the air. *Help! Over here!*

Over Here

Jopa! I hiss and hardpress down his arms.
Stop! But it's too late. The figure beside
the fire draws a gun, then stands in attack
position. I know for sure we've been spotted when whoever it is barrels toward us
like a living missile.

Missile

Get down! I throw myself over Jopa, over D-39 with speed and force. My heart whip-rattles, and I don't know why we aren't running, why I haven't pulled out the screwdriver. I think of Papa fussing at me in the looganut fields. *Faster, Klynt.* But I'm not fast, I'm slow, because D-39 is barely operational, and getting worse each moment. Better to hunker down, take whatever is coming. So I imagine myself as a mother hen, fluffing my feathers over my chicks. We could try to run, but I know we would fail.

Fail

The boots stop right in front of my face. Boots with laces, thank goodness. Not roboboots. Relief loosens my shoulders only slightly, because the barrel of a gun is in front of my nose. So close that I can smell the gunpowder. *Who are you?* a voice asks, and I peek up and out. I don't answer right away, because if this is a test, I don't want to fail it. It's a woman—a soldier who looks to be about as old as Tiev, though it's hard to tell for sure when her gun is pointed at my head. D-39 whines, and she slings the gun aside. *You've got a robodog?*

She crouches, holsters her weapon, and holds out her hand for D-39 to sniff. When he licks her fingers, my whole body goes slack. This soldier could have killed us already, but she's petting D-39 instead. We may be weak, tired, and hungry, but we're alive. We're okay.

Okay

Jopa pops up like he used to, before the
sleeping drugs. *I'm Jopa, and this is Klynt.
Our parents and Tiev* . . . His words drop
off as he brushes hair out of his eyes. *We
don't know where they are, so we're going to
Everlake. Until the deathstretch is over.* He
says it like all is okay, like we know where
we're going, like this strange woman is a
new friend we've just met at a community
picnic. Like this journey, this encounter,
is all perfectly normal.

Normal

The soldier, who I can now see is wearing a navy blue government uniform rather than the Patriots' rich green, pauses and sweettalks D-39.

How can she work for President Vex? I thought anyone who supported our government must be an uncaring, unfeeling monster. But this woman. She seems kind, compassionate. Normal. She smells sweet, like oranges. When my eyes meet hers, I think she gets it. She's checking in with me, being sure not to say anything that might disturb Jopa.

I offer the soldier a tiny quirk, and she returns it. She shifts her gun so that it hangs over her back and lowers herself to the ground. She nuzzles D-39 nose-to-nose, like he belongs to her. *You shouldn't be out here alone*, she says. *It's too dangerous.* I stroke D-39's back and repeat the words I told Papa. *We're not alone. We have D-39.* A sluggish D-39, but still.

Still

Good dog, the woman croons, lifting D-39's chin to examine his chestplate. *Makes me miss my DogE 2.0.* I lift my eyebrows. The DogE 2.0 is a brand that's the opposite of D-39. All slick metal, no fur anywhere. No eating or pooping. Much more modern.

When she spots the Dog Alive logo, she whistles. *Wow, I've never seen one of these up close. It's even more real-looking than I imagined.* She smooths the silk on the inside of D-39's scratchpatched ear. *So,* Jopa says, *what happened to him? Your DogE 2.0?*

The soldier quirkfaces at Jopa, but her eyes stay puddleglum. *Same thing that happens to all robos.* She cocks her head as one of D-39's indicator lights flickers. She hard-presses her ear to the chestplate, listening for something. *What?* I say. *Do you know what's wrong with him?*

She shakes her head. *Hmmm.* She looks into D-39's eyes as she runs her hands along his legs. She shakes her head again.

What? Jopa says, and I grab his hand. The soldier looks from Jopa to me, and back again. *I'm sorry*, she says and puts a hand on her gun. My heart thudjams, and I get that prickletwitch feeling again. I don't want to know what she's sorry for. And I don't want her kind of help. I turn my back to her as I wrap my arms around D-39's neck. I'm still in charge here, and I won't let her take him from me. *He stays with me.*

With Me

The soldier lifts her hands. *Hey, hey. Easy now. I didn't mean—* Her words hang in the air as some shots ring out. Quicker than a prairie rattler, she leaps from the ground and swings the gun into her hands. *You can't stay out here*, she says without looking at us. *And you can't come with me. Fighting is coming this way.* She pulls a device from her holster. *Where is this Everlake?*

In the Wilds, Jopa starts. *We just have to find the blue—* I grab Jopa's hand. *No, Jopa.* Everlake is a secret place. I don't know if we should tell someone who works for the government where it is. How do I know if I can trust her? More shots ring out, closer this time. I'm about to tell the soldier to leave, we'll be fine, but then D-39 lifts his head and licks her fingers. And she lets him.

If D-39 trusts her, then so can I. If she's good with a robo slipslopping her fingers, then she can't be all bad.

All Bad

I pull out my map. *Across the border*, I sweetmurmur, my voice raspy and dry. *Here*. I point out the faint star. She cocks her head. *That's a long way*. My heart motors. *Only thirty more miles, right? We can do that in two or three days*. Or at least we could have. Before D-39 started acting so weird. The soldier shakes her head. *Not thirty miles. More like fifty*. My chest fills with flutterbugs. *But*— How can that be? *It's only forty miles from where we live, and we've been walking for two days already*. Jopa peels a sock back from his heel. *I've got blisters to prove it*. The soldier comes out of her attack stance to show us the screen on her device. *I don't know about all that. But according to this, it's fifty miles from here*. I find the flashing green light that shows where we are and measure it against the red dot where Everlake is. I can't help it: I almost dripface.

Dripface

Instead of north, we've been traveling west. *How did we go the wrong way?* No one answers. But we did. How else would we be back near the fighting?

I grab Jopa's hand. How can I admit that I screwed up? *Jopa,* I sweetmurmur. *I'm sorry.* His head hangs so that his chin nearly touches his chest. *It's too far,* he says. A tear splashes from his eye onto the top of D-39's head. My robo doesn't even look up.

I swallow. How did this happen? I guess I didn't learn as much from Papa about navigation as I thought. I don't know why Jopa or D-39 or anyone would follow me when I've made so many mistakes.

Mistakes

Jopa listens as I explain how we walked the wrong way. *Look*, the soldier says, *you just have to keep going.* She grabs my shoulders. *It's really important. You and the—* She swallows as more gunfire erupts, even closer to us than before. *You and your robo. You can't stop now. It's too dangerous. And there's too much at stake.*

I whipwhirl away from her. What if D-39 really is military like Papa thought? One thing's for certain: I don't need a soldier or anyone to tell me it's dangerous. Our lives are at stake. And also, because of her and others like her, our freedom is at stake.

My breath hitches. I'm so flipfurious that we've been going the wrong way. And D-39 is itchglitching, and Jopa has blisters, and we're hungry and cold and wet and— *Listen*, the soldier says. *It doesn't matter now. You made a mistake. So what?* She points at D-39 and Jopa. *This is your main concern now. Getting to safety. Getting him well and healthy. Getting him home. All creatures deserve to be in a place where they feel safe.*

Safe

Jopa leans against me. *I'm tired, K-K. Home sounds good.* I rub his shoulders. *I know, Jopa. I know.* The soldier reaches into her pack. *Do you have any water?* I show her the empty grocery sack. *No.*

Here. She slides her canteen strap over her head. It's old-school—disc-shaped thermos with a screw-top lid. It would make a fine addition to my Museum of Fond Memories. *Now listen carefully. There's a supply station just a few miles from here. You'll be safe there. Dr. Wesl will help you. Okay? But you need to hurry.*

Thanks. My eyes bigsky. *No problem*, she says. *Promise me you'll stop at the supply station. Find Dr. Wesl, okay? He'll help you get to safety.* I nod, and she flashes a quick quirk. No one has to say out loud that she's moving on.

Moving On

The soldier lipbrushes D-39's nose, and his eyes shutterbug. When her device beeps, her face turns stern. *Now, go. I didn't see you, and you didn't see me.* She takes a step, then turns back to us. *Seriously, be careful. You're on the front lines of a deathstretch. Trust no one. And you tell Dr. Wesl—* She shrugs. *Never mind.* Jopa grabs her hand. *Wait!* he says. *What's your name?*

Name

The soldier freezes. Quirkfaces. *Nuni. My name is Nuni.* As she jogs away, getting smaller and smaller by the second, Jopa digs in the pack, pulls out his ants. *Nuni, wait! I want to show you my ants!*

And that's right when it happens. From somewhere, from everywhere, from nowhere—POP, POP, POP! A different kind of gunshot. My mouth gapes as Nuni falls to the ground.

Ground

My breath hitches, disappears as I slam my arm against Jopa's back to flatten him onto the ground beside D-39. So he won't see what just happened to Nuni.

But it's too late. Jopa knows exactly what happened. *Nuni*, he breathes, his face hard-pressed against D-39's side. I don't have to see it to know he's dripfacing. My mind reels, repeats. Nuni running, Nuni falling. Nuni running, Nuni falling.

The pop-shots still ring in my ears when BOOM! A boomblast roars beside us, so close my chest heaves. Every cell tingles like I'm coming apart, and I think the whole world might explode.

Explode

Earth quiverquakes; leafgiants fly. Rubble
pummels my back and my legs. My lungs
become a net that catches only smoke. My
world no longer my world, it's more like a
shaken cold-dust globe. My ears ring. I can't
hear Jopa or D-39. My eyes fill with dirt-
dust, smoke, terror. All I can think: *Mama.*
We're so close, Mama. Show me a light!

Light

After I don't know how long, Mama's voice comes to me feathery as goose down. *Klynt. Get up, Klynt.*

A memory of her dimpled cheek flashes behind my eyes. A sudden sun bright, so bright. *There you are!*

Her arms pulling me from my long-ago hiding place under the table, my heart beating against her heart. *Here I am.*

Here I Am

I'm still breathing. With both Jopa and D-39 beside me. *You okay?* I run my hands down Jopa's arms and legs, checking to see if he's in one piece. He is. He really is. I do the same with D-39, and he, too, is whole. A sound comes out of my throat—half snickergiggle, half sob, as quiverquakes wrack my body. Jopa's eyes bigsky, and he opens his mouth to say something. *Shhh*, I say. *Stay down.*

It's like I'm a robo and my programming has an itchglitch. Even though my animal brain screams *run*, my gut holds a cannonball that won't budge. The explosion blasted us a ways from where we talked with Nuni. I can't even look over to where Nuni dropped to the ground. I'm not sure now which direction it was. *I need a jinglesnap*, I tell Jopa. *The boomblast fatrattled my bearings.*

When a troop of robosoldiers appears at the edge of the field, I almost can't breathe. *Please*, I pray. *Please go away.* I don't know if God hears me, but I know D-39 does, because he licks my hand. We wait a minute—feels like an hour, a day—and finally the robos move. They melt away like cold-dustflakes do when the ground is still warm. One moment there. The next one, gone.

Gone

We wait on the ground for a long time after the soldiers disappear—so long that daylight turns to twilight and a blusterblow whipwhirls sharp and cold. Jopa quiverquakes beside me, even though I tucked him into the afghan, even though D-39 pants beside us.

My ants, Jopa says. *They're gone.* He sniffles, coughs. I upcuddle him to me. *I know.* If only he hadn't taken them out of the pack, they might still be with us. But there's nothing to be done about it now. *It will be okay. We'll find more ants, right? They're survivors. Like us.* It's what I've been telling myself ever since we saw the first flying robofighters.

Fifty more miles to Everlake. I don't know how we're going to do it. All I know is we've got to get there before freezeseason puts us in a stranglehold. Before all three of us end up sick.

Sick

D-39, I croon, and I stroke his muzzle. I scan my memory for anything Gloria at the pit might have mentioned about itch-glitches in the Dog Alive robos, and what to do about it. Sure, D-39 needs m-fuel. But this seems different. My robo licks my face with his usual tenderness, but it's in slow-mo, and his polka-dotted tongue is drier than usual. His motor hums steady as anything. Surely the programmers didn't add actual illness to his code in addition to the eating and pooping?

I sigh beneath the darkening sky. Hopefully D-39 feels better after this rest. So many things I don't understand, so much I want to learn. I can't process everything that's happened on this day, except that we're not any closer to our destination. We've got to take advantage of even the smallest sliver of daylight. *Jopa?* I gently shake his shoulder. *We can't sleep yet. The only way to get to Everlake is to keep going.* He lifts his arms, and I pull him to his feet. *Let's walk. Just for a little while.*

A Little While

Jopa rubs his belly. *And then we'll eat?* I nod. *And then we'll eat.* We lift out of the grass, all ear-twitch and caution, like foxes or bison. It takes D-39 a minute to get going. *Good boy*, I coax, and he pushes forward. He pants, heavy tongue lolling out of his mouth like he's tired, so tired. If only I had some m-fuel. Or whatever it is he needs. I'm a tinkerer, and I don't know how to fix him. His mechanics don't make sense. They never have. I think it's a small miracle when somehow he stays with us, step by step by step.

Step by Step

We don't stop until we are deep in the woods. Papa always calls it the bush. It's like the inbetweenlands that separate the Worselands from the Wilds.

We ration the water inside the canteen Nuni gave us, but it isn't enough. Soon there are only a few drops left. D-39 pants so hard watching us drink that I'm sure this time he'll take some, but he doesn't. *Why isn't he drinking?* Jopa asks. I shake my head, exasperated. *I wish I knew!* He may be a robo, but it's awful to see his eyes turn glassy and his paws drag. *It's probably his programming*, I say. *Maybe it's all gone gobbledegook from age and lack of good maintenance.*

Or, Jopa says, *the river*. My heart fist-clenches, because I thought of that, too. I just didn't want to say it. *I know*, I say. *That's the last time D-39 drank anything.* As the sky darkens, we push forward. When a leafgiant creaks in the blusterblow, Jopa jumps like it's a gunshot.

Not D-39. He flops onto the ground, his eyelids shutterbugging, and his breath in whifflegusts, like he's been running for hours. I stroke his neck. *Oh, D-39.* I try to keep the desperation and startle-spook out of my voice, but it doesn't work. *What's wrong?*

What's Wrong?

D-39 lifts his head and hacks up water and rabbit-rot. I pull him with me away from the puddle, away from the stench, but he does it again and again. Jopa strokes his back, sing-songs the ant species. *Carpenter, harvester, weaver, fire . . . Carpenter, harvester, weaver, fire . . .*

As much as I don't want to stop walking forward, I know we must. We're all too tired, and it's dark now. I switch D-39 into sleepmode and hope it helps. *Okay*, I say. *We'll rest here until morning.*

Morning

When light finally breaks, it's hard to unfold from the cocoon of Jopa's afghan. My head throbs from hunger, and my body is stiff from the cold. Jopa wakes slowly. First his eyes crack open. He lies there, eyes shutterbugging before he moves any other part of his body. *You okay?* I ask. I'm relieved when he nods and upcuddles closer to me.

D-39 doesn't wiggle or quirkface or jerk-wag his tail. He can't even lift his head. As soon as Jopa sees him, he strokes his ears and sings one of his antsongs. *When ants go home, they count their steps, count their steps, count their steps. When ants go home, they count their steps, early in the morning.* The song gets stuck in my head. *Is that true, Jopa? Do ants really count their steps?*

Jopa tells me it really is true and launches into a long explanation about the experiments scientists did to find out. When he finally takes a breath, he checks in again on D-39. *It's so weird*, he says. *Like D-39 is broken.*

Broken

I pull D-39's head into my lap, tip the canteen, and shake. But it's empty now. No water. *Come on, D-39.* He just closes his eyes. Whatever it is that's making him itchglitchy isn't fixing itself. *Oh, D-39.* He doesn't even lick at me. If only I knew more about how to repair broken robos. *Jopa,* I say, *Everlake will have to wait. First we need to get to the supply station Nuni told us about. To get D-39 some help.*

Help

I stroke D-39's ears one last time before flipping the hood up on my coat. The air smells like cold-dust, and D-39 looks like salvage. He can't walk. As much as I hate it, we'll have to drag him. He's not strong enough to make it on his own. I swallow. Please, God, let my robo be okay. And if we run up on anyone today, let them be friendly like Nuni.

While I'm busy worrying about D-39, we can't forget that we're in a deathstretch zone. Soldiers, guns, boomblasts—they could be anywhere. *It can't be too much farther*, I say aloud. What I mean is, it better not be too much farther. The time is now to cover some ground, and also help my robo. To remember all the things Papa taught me, though I feel far more like a student than an expert. Now it's time to resume my role as teacher.

Teacher

My stomach growls as I pull the bedsheet and coil of rope from my pack. *Like this*, I say, and show Jopa how to tie a bowline. It takes both of us half rolling, half pulling to move D-39 onto our makeshift gurney. When we finally get him settled, I have to take a moment to breathe. *It's going to be okay*, I sweetmurmur to D-39. Please, let my armslegsshoulders carry him, I pray. Please let the knots hold.

Knots Hold

Here I am, like Papa predicted, needing a knot I'd never have known how to tie if not for him. A lump comes into my throat as I once again remember the day we visited Gloria's salvage pit, how Papa zapjawed me by letting me keep D-39.

So often I've felt like Papa cared more about the looganuts than he cared about me. But wasn't that love, when he let me keep my robo? And later in the burrow, when he tried to cast out D-39, he was so, so sorry. What if that was love, too? Maybe there are thousands, millions of ways to show love.

I may not always like Papa's ways, but maybe that's how he says he values me without actually saying it. Like me and Jopa tying a knot to drag D-39 across the bush. Right now, this moment, I want to love like Papa.

Like Papa

He's so heavy, Jopa says as he discards the afghan. His breath comes out in short little huffs, quick like mine. *Hey*, I say. *Why don't you be in charge of the pack? We'll be faster that way*. He releases his grip on the bedsheet and shoulders the pack. *Just stay close*. I bet those are the words Papa would say to me if he were here.

My leg muscles burn as we walk-shuffle-slide. Sometimes the sheet gets hung up on rocks and branches. Other times we go for long stretches when the sheet rustles reassuringly against smooth ground. When we come to a small lake that looks clean, I don't want to stop, but I know if Papa were here, he would stop. So we do, and we use the water filter to fill Nuni's canteen. And then we start walking again.

When the scent of something burning teases my nostrils, I put Jopa in charge of scouting for smoke. Papa warned me that surprises can be deadly. The more we know, the more we pay attention, the better off we'll be.

By afternoon we're so deep into the bush that we haven't seen a house or building for hours. The worst is how unresponsive D-39 is. I miss his tail swishswiping and his head bumping my thigh. It's tough going, way worse than anything I've ever done in the looganut fields. My throat turns sandpapery, and the gloves can't keep the rope from burning my hands. Even my head aches from the weight of D-39 and the coldsnap of loneliness.

Loneliness

I drag D-39 across steep, jagged rocks, my muscles screaming. But I don't stop. *Carpenter ants travel as far as one hundred yards for food*, Jopa says. *They go about three inches per second*. I quirkface. *Good to know we're at least going as fast as an ant*. I press forward, my footsteps making barely a murmur, as if I am prey in a land thick with wolves.

But I'm not prey. I am the *wolf*. A lonely wolf missing part of her pack. I am a girl with a robo, traveling with a boy who is strong, stronger, strongEST. We carry a screwdriver and slingshot, and we sing, even if no one can hear our voices.

Voices

Men's voices, deep and corncob rough. I grab Jopa's hand and dive behind a boulder. My breath is as loud as the chug-chug to my own ears. D-39 whines, but it is such a soft sound I think not even Jopa hears it. We're quiet, so quiet, but that can't change the fact that while the bedsheet may be ripped and smudged, it's still I-spy white.

The men swagger in too-big boots, scuffed rifles and rounds of ammunition hanging across their backs and chests. No uniforms, just regular clothes that hang on some, too tight on others. Probably pilfered from the dead. Their bushy beards and hair remind me of the lion-man. But this is not one man. It's five. A pack.

My gut says they will hurt us, not help us. So I decide we will not run, because we can only walk-shuffle-slide. *Shhh*, I tell Jopa, and he makes a motion of zipzipping his lip. We are both learning. This time we will not call out, even though D-39 is sick and we are all famished and exhausted.

No. We will wait.

Wait

The men are not in a hurry. Not only do they have weapons, one carries a string of rabbits and another carries a basket of what I can smell is fish. Oh, what I wouldn't give for a nice piece of fish!

Jopa closes his eyes while we wait for them to get out of eyesight and earshot. Before the men have turned to specks, Jopa nods off. His head rests on the pack, and a small snore escapes his lips.

My robo is so quiet I must lay an ear against his chestplate to feel the vibration of his internal fan. Or is that my own heartbeat in my ears? It isn't steady like the sound of a motor. More like a flutterbug with damp, weak wings. Yes, moving. But barely.

Barely

By moonrise the men are long gone, and so are we. It's tempting to follow their prints, because maybe they are more experienced at following directions. Maybe they know the exact path to wherever they're headed. But we don't want to risk running up on them again. And I think this time we're going the right way.

My shoulder blades are as unbending as shovels, and I have to stop, just for a jinglesnap. When I check in on D-39, he barely looks up and his head lies in a pool of chugspew. *When did that happen?* I ask Jopa. He pinches his nose against the sour smell. *I don't know*, he says in a voice that sounds digital. We are no longer two humans and a robo. We have become something scarcely recognizable.

Scarcely Recognizable

My body, not my body. A planet circling a
deepdark star.

My tongue, not my tongue. A small stone
covered in moss.

My arms, not my arms. Dead deer left to
dry in the shadow of a leafgiant.

My legs, not my legs. Oak logs that I can
only drag.

Drag

My thoughts whipwhirl to Mama. Where is she? What is she doing?

Mama, I don't know where we are or what time it is or how long it's been. Just like the pie ticktock inside Jopa's burrow, I have no numbers to mark our progress. Only sunrise, sunset. Time drags.

Light slips into the hand of night without asking permission—it seems nothing and no one asks permission anymore—and we sleepstagger through fogsteam into another world.

Another World

Look! Jopa points toward a stand of evergreen leafgiants. And then I see it: the rise of a tent, smoke curling into the air above the leafgiants, maybe a hundred yards from us. *Is that the supply station?* I ask Jopa, but he doesn't answer. I'm pretty sure it is, because it looks exactly like Nuni described. *One way to find out*, I say with faux confidence. *It's gotta be*, Jopa says. So we shift into high gear, eager to get there.

My heart thudjams and all my muscles scream as my legs strain to reach the tent as quickly as possible. D-39 has only gotten heavier as the day has progressed. Please don't let this world be some sort of mirage! As two figures race toward us, I instinctively suck in my breath and reach for D-39. As glad as I am that we've found other humans, Nuni's words echo in my mind: *Trust no one.* But I'm too tired to be suspicious, and D-39 is too sick. *Hold up your hands*, I instruct Jopa. *Just to be safe.* I don't know if it will work, but doesn't everyone know the universal sign for surrender?

Surrender

No one is more zapjawed than I am when
the soldiers arrive, hands in the air like
ours. Their uniforms are not blue or green,
but white. One sleeve marked with a red
"T" for techie, the other with a stitched
olive branch and the words *Peace Brigade*.

Peace Brigade

I know from the streamscreen that Peace Brigade techies are neutral—they don't work for the government or the Patriots. Their job is to help everyone. As we follow them to the tent, I see it isn't one tent, but two. They flank an old hunting cabin. Deer racks still adorn the walls, and the techies use them to store robo parts and medical supplies marked with the olive-branch insignia. When I turn around, I realize we've walked past armed guards on either side of the door. A string of bare bulbs lights the interior, and I can hear the purr of a generator. *Please*, I say. Between the dryness of my throat and the dropping temperature, I can barely form words. My mind has turned to fogsteam. *My robo.*

My Robo

The guards don't pull their guns. They push open the door as two techies lift D-39 onto a makeshift gurney and usher us inside. I shutterbug against the flickering lights and the buzz of techies as they tend to various machines. There are drones and robos and tables strewn with pieces I don't know how they will ever put back together. It reminds me of my old room, before the boomblast. My Museum of Fond Memories.

My chest tightens as we follow the techies into a room marked "Triage." I know from Mama's vet books that that's the name for an area where it's decided who needs what kind of help most urgently. I pull Jopa close to me. *They're the experts. We can trust them to help D-39, right?* His reply may be intended as a sweetmurmur, but it comes out loud. *But Nuni said—* Before he can complete his sentence, a bearded man in a white lab coat looks up from a chart. *I'm sorry, but I couldn't help overhearing you.* His eyes meet mine. *I'm Dr. Wesl. Did you say Nuni?*

I nod. Dr. Wesl! He drops the chart, grabs my arm. *Have you seen her? Is she okay?* I focus on the first question. *Yes.* We definitely saw her. *She said you'd help us. You'd fix my robo.* His cheeks lift, and he holds out his hand.

His Hand

His hand covers my poor, beat-up hand like a blanket, instantly bringing relief and comfort. It's a firm handshake, the kind Papa taught me. His eyes glimmerspark with real warmth and sincerity. *Any friend of Nuni's is a friend of mine.*

She— My mind fills with an image of how Nuni lipbrushed D-39's nose. *She really liked D-39.* Hardly a sweetmurmur, my throat is so dry. Dr. Wesl fills in the blanks. *I bet she did. That girl loves robodogs. And I'm going to take care of this one, I guarantee.*

Guarantee

Humans first, Dr. Wesl says. *I know you're worried about the robo, but I need to look at you and your brother.*

Friend, I correct. Though I'd be lucky to have Jopa for a brother. *Please be quick.* As he checks Jopa's heartrate and lifts his eyelids to shine a penlight into his eyes, I answer his questions about where we're from and how we know each other. *Water, antibiotics, stat*, he orders and settles Jopa into a cushioned chair. Jopa practically melts, he's so tired. I push the hair back from his forehead. *H_2O, coming right up*, I tell him, wishing I could promise more guarantees. He smiles a sleepy smile, eyes already closing.

While Jopa naps, it's my turn to get checked. Dr. Wesl instructs me to breathe deep, and I do. Finally he puts all his tools away and turns to me. *You're dehydrated, exhausted.* He points at the blisters and rope burns on my hands and shoulders. *Some abrasions, a little banged up. But you are otherwise fine.*

Fine

Dr. Wesl keeps talking as he lifts D-39 onto the table. Not quizzing me now so much as distracting me from my worries. *Hi, D-39*, he says as he examines my robo's chestplate. *Nuni keeps saying after all this is over, we're going to get a whole fleet of robos.* His quirk reveals a gap between his front teeth. His voice drops to a sweetmurmur. *Just between you and me, I've always been more of a cat man. But if Nuni wants another dog—* I break his gaze and turn toward Jopa. Partly to check on him—he's still sleeping—but mostly because Dr. Wesl thinks Nuni is fine. But I can't tell him what happened to Nuni. Not yet.

He watches the monitor lights shutterbug and listens to the motor hum. He adds m-fuel. He whips an electrical cord deep from his labcoat pocket and plugs one side into the port on D-39's chestplate and the other to a streamscreen. Right away the streamscreen starts filling with code. And then, just as suddenly, it stops. Stops. Dr. Wesl catches his breath. The code disappears, and all that's left on the screen is a cursor, shutterbugging green.

What is it? I ask. *What's wrong?* He glances at the door where two techies stand, and when his voice comes, it's louder than it needs to be. *I'm so sorry. This one's a goner.*

Goner

See? Dr. Wesl points to the screen. *Robo's flatlining as we speak. Nothing to stop it from bzzflopping now.* He rips the cord from D-39's chestplate. *No!* I cry. Not my robo! Not D-39! I hurryscurry to his side. *He's fine. He has to be fine.*

I'm sorry, Dr. Wesl says again, softly this time, just to me. It's like I've been mauled by a runaway chug-chug. What does he mean he's sorry? I whipwhirl around, and for once I'm glad Jopa is sleeping. I don't want him to hear this. No one should have to hear this. And maybe if no one hears it, it won't be true.

Dr. Wesl instructs the techies to keep quiet, for Jopa. *His body's had enough shock for now.* Then louder, he announces, *I'll walk the girl down to the scrap room. So she can give her robo a proper goodbye.*

Goodbye

Goodbye. That word explodes like a boomblast inside my chest. I want to follow my robo and fast. *Wait,* I say. I want to throw myself on top of D-39 and show Dr. Wesl he's wrong.

But I can't. I can't leave Jopa. I reach to wake him, but Dr. Wesl stops me. *He needs to sleep.* I know that. Of course I know that. *Not without me.*

Dr. Wesl's eyes bigsky with understanding, and he flips a switch on the wall. *Will this help?* Cameras capture images of Jopa at various angles, and all of it shows up on a small device that Dr. Wesl hardpresses into my palm. *You don't have to worry. If he so much as wiggles, you can be back in two seconds. We're going down just one floor.*

His voice turns deeper, more insistent. *He needs to sleep, and you need to come with me.* I look at the device, the cameras, Jopa, and back again. He does need the sleep. I know he does. *Just one floor down?* Dr. Wesl nods. *Yes. Now, come on, let's go to the basement.*

The Basement

I'll be back, I sweetmurmur to Jopa as we leave the room. I know Jopa will understand, even though I promised I'd stay by his side. Right now Jopa is fine, but D-39 is not.

Oh, my D-39! My fingers curl around his matted, dirty neck fur. My robo can't bzz-flop. Not now. Not after all this!

Dr. Wesl leads us onto an elevator, rolling D-39 along on a cart. I realize how misleading this supply center is. You'd never suspect by looking at the tent-and-cabin structure on the outside that it has a basement.

I snatch Dr. Wesl's hand. *You've got to do something! Nuni said—* As soon as the doors close and we're alone in the elevator, he grabs my shoulders. *Listen, kid. You've got to pull yourself together. I can't help you or the D-39 if you don't play your part. Okay? Everything you're feeling you've got to shove down deep inside you. No words at all, okay? For this to work, you* must *stay silent.*

Silent

As we exit the elevator into a hallway, it's hard to stay silent. What I want is to ask more questions. What does Dr. Wesl mean, *my part?* If I have a part, I sure don't know what it is.

But I can tell Dr. Wesl means business, and the corridor is swarming with techies, so I shove my questions down deep with my feelings. I check the monitor to look in on Jopa. Still sleeping. I listen to Dr. Wesl greet a new team of techies and explain about D-39 bzzflopping. I cover my ears with my hands. I can't listen. I want to focus on my robo. My sweet, beautiful D-39.

It isn't until we get into the scrap room that things change. It smells of oil and metal. The walls are lined with floor-to-ceiling shelves loaded with spare parts, batteries, and electronic chips—a restoration expert's dream! But I can hardly think about that now. Not when Dr. Wesl's voice turns zap-jawed. *I can't believe this.* I stand back as he removes a few screws, then carefully lifts a strip of metal from D-39's back. He does the same with the solar panel and the m-fuel tank, and it's like D-39 is shrinking before my eyes. Finally he grabs the hummingbird motor. Pulls it right off. *Click-click-click*, the screws pop.

My eyes bigsky. *What are you doing?* It's like he's stripping away D-39's skin— except he's not. I still see fur. *Wow*, Dr. Wesl says. *This is fantastic! I've never seen anything like this.*

This

Stop! I scream. *You'll break him.* Dr. Wesl
looks at me. *Him? This isn't a him. It's a
her. A female.* Hey hi ho there. *A what?* He
quirkfaces. *Didn't you know? This isn't a
robo. It's a real dog* disguised *as a robo.* My
head feels marshmallow-light. Real? D-39
is a *real* dog?

Real Dog

I can't breathe. I can't comprehend what Dr. Wesl is saying. *If she's going to have any chance*, he continues, *we've got to get her out of this casing.*

I can do nothing but watch as the rest of the metal and molded plastic shell clatters to the floor. There's a dog under there. A real dog. My D-39 is *real*.

I've heard about dogs being disguised as robos to cross the border, Dr. Wesl says, *but I've never actually seen one. The decoy motor actually burns m-fuel. Everything works just like a robo. It's amazing!* My mind whipwhirls and my legs go rubbersoft. I hold on to the table to steady myself. I need to understand this. *You mean someone rearranged the robo parts, shaped them into a coat of armor?* Dr. Wesl's face is bright with excitement. *That's right. And instead of mounting it on a metal frame, what's underneath is a real, breathing dog.* I can't believe it.

And then I do. Because it explains everything. The eating and the sickness and the
way D-39 saved me that time in the river
and the softness of his—her—ears and
even the time he—*she*—accidentally bit
Papa. My robo isn't a robo at all. She's real!

Hi, D-39, Dr. Wesl says. *You're definitely in
the right place.*

Right Place

I check the monitor again to see how Jopa is doing. Still sleeping. He is going to go jayballs when he finds out about D-39!

Dr. Wesl quickly examines D-39 by listening to his heart—*her* heart—with a stethoscope. How long will it take me to absorb this new information? Dr. Wesl shines a light in D-39's eyes and pinches her skin. *Dehydrated*, he says, *like you. And she's running a fever. Likely an infection. Or some sort of bacteria she picked up.* My chest fistclenches. *BrkX?*

Dr. Wesl shakes his head. *No, no, nothing like that.* I finger the rawfire places where the plastic plating was attached. Her skin is red and swollen.

My heart thudjams. All this time I was thinking of tech stuff to make D-39 better—all that m-fuel that could have been used for other things! I wasn't thinking about medical stuff at all. Thank goodness we made it to the right place and right person. *What can you do to make her better? Give her some medicine?*

Medicine

Yes, Dr. Wesl says. *But we'll have to be careful. Keep this as contained as possible. Which means you and Jopa can stay upstairs in my office, but D-39 needs to stay down here. She needs a round of antibiotics, among other things.*

As Dr. Wesl pulls out a tube of ointment to treat D-39's raw spots, I hold out my hand. *Let me do it*, I say. I may not be a medical expert, but that's only because no one's taught me yet.

Once we get her all doctored, I wash my hands and check the monitor. Jopa's beginning to stir. I can't wait to tell him about D-39!

I skip the elevator and take the stairs two at a time to reach Jopa. I'm breathless when I get there. *Jopa*, I say and stroke his arm. His eyelids flutter. *Tiev?*

No, Jopa. It's me, Klynt. He quirkfaces. *K-K.* I stroke his cheek. *I've got something to tell you. You're not going to believe it, Jopa. It's completely jayballs.*

Jayballs

Jopa pushes the hair off his forehead. *Did we make it? Are we at Everlake?* I shake my head. *Not yet. But Jopa, D-39—* I want to tell him everything. What do I tell him first? I take a breath to force myself to slow down. *Jopa. D-39 is not a robo. She's real.*

Jopa's brow creases, and I nod my head. *It's true. D-39 is a real dog.* His eyes bigsky. *Real like my ants?* I quirkface. *Yes. Real like you and me.*

Jopa goes jayballs. Comes out of his seat, questions jumping out of his mouth like popcorn. Like the old Jopa. By the time Dr. Wesl comes back into the room with soup and wheatkin crackers, I've got him all caught up.

As Jopa slurps soup mouth-to-bowl, the doctor closes the door so that it's just us three. *How did you get a real dog? And how'd she get so sick? It's time to tell me what happened.*

What Happened

I tell Dr. Wesl about how D-39 appeared one day at our farm and about what Gloria said at the pit and the boomblasts and the burrows and finally the river. How it was filled with dead things, and I wasn't quick enough to stop D-39 from drinking.

And you didn't know she was real? he asks. *You're not part of the K-9 Corridor?* My eyes go all bigsky. Jopa's do, too. It's starting to make sense—all the things that are different about D-39. Oh, Papa! D-39 is not military at all! That's why she barked and ate and slipslopped and paced and whined. Because she's *real*! Part of me swells with pride. By some accident, I have become part of the K-9 Corridor. Like Mama.

Like Mama

I sniffle and quirkface at the same time.
D-39 is real! This whole time I've been
helping save a flesh-and-blood dog. I've
been playing a part in something big and
important, without even knowing it.

And then it hits me. I should have known.
I would have taken such better care if I
had known! *I'm sorry*, I sweetmurmur.

Sorry? Dr. Wesl says. *Are you kidding? You're a
hero! D-39's infection and the deathstretch—
none of it is your fault.*

Fault

A hero. Me? With all the mistakes I've made? My voice, when it finally comes, snapcrackles like ice. *Will she be okay?*

We'll do what we can. His quirk is both kind and puddleglum at the same time. *Come on. I'll take you back down to see her.* Dr. Wesl leads us to the scrap room in the basement.

D-39 looks different, now that I know she's a she. And smaller, more fragile without the casing. I can actually see her chest moving up and down with each breath.

See? I say to Jopa. His quirkface is so big as he places a hand on her side. *She's breathing*, he says. *She really is real!*

As Dr. Wesl tells us again how brave we are, I swallow. I know I should tell him what happened to Nuni, and how it's kind of our fault. He deserves to know. But not now. Not yet.

Right now what she needs is a drip. Dr. Wesl pulls two vials and a needle from a back cabinet. From a box marked "spare parts" he grabs a bag of fluid that looks like the one that was attached to Jopa. *No!* I throw myself on top of my dog. *Not D-39! She's all we've got!*

All We've Got

My heart doesn't stop ramscrambling until Dr. Wesl explains that the drip is temporary. It will restore D-39's energy and immune system more quickly. Yes, it's medication, but it's not the sleeping kind. *Antibiotics. For the infection*, he tells me. *It's all we've got during the deathstretch.* It will drip, drip, drip like freshwash to hopefully jumpstart the process of healing.

Healing

Dr. Wesl knows that I want to stay with D-39, and Jopa wants to stay with me, so he offers us warm washcloths, towels, fresh clothes. Right there in the scrap room. We eat more steaming soup, and there's even a dish of butter to go with the wheatkins.

After we're done Jopa leans into me, yawns. *Read to me?* I lift my eyebrows. No books. *How about I tell you a story instead?* He consents, and I tell him about a girl who hates the farm until one day, she climbs a looganut stalk, and it lifts her all the way to the sun. *Like our skysail*, he says. His eyes close, and I tell him how some-day that skysail will rise in a sky without boomblasts. We'll watch it dance with the clouds, whole and floating.

Floating

Belly full, I sleep. I dream of looganuts, their yellow faces drifting around me, floating like hotseason clouds. When I wake, I stroke D-39.

I sleep, she sleeps. Her still body every so often animates with soft whines and moving paws as she dreams of whatever real dogs dream of. *Better*, Dr. Wesl says. I squeeze my eyes shut and quirkface. Hey hi ho there. If you're listening, Mama, D-39 is better!

Better

The deathstretch has made me uncertain about everything, but also I'm better at relishing even the smallest moment. I don't all the way believe D-39's going to make it until the next morning when I stroke her silky ear that feels so much smaller and warmer than the old scratchpatched one. When D-39 oh-so-gently licks my cheek, I can't stop quirkfacing.

Quirkfacing

We don't talk about D-39 being a real dog.
Dr. Wesl says we have to keep it quiet for
her safety. We split our time between his
office and the scrap room, where D-39 stays
in a crate.

We tell the techies I'm trying to refurbish
my robo by using some of their many retro
replacement parts. I do, in fact, plunder
the parts and slap a few pieces together. It
allows me to be close to D-39, and it gives
me an excuse to use my screwdriver.

The techies are more entertained by Jopa
anyway. They give him a new jar, and even
though there are no ants in it yet, it's
enough to get Jopa quirkfacing again as he
rattles off random ant facts to anyone who
will listen.

And after a week of soft food and medicine and me reading to her, D-39 is nearly
recovered, too. The rawfire places on her
skin have healed over and hair is starting
to grow. I can feel myself getting itchy,
ready to continue on our journey.

Journey

One afternoon Jopa and D-39 and I use the old stairs near the back entrance to sneak outside. I shiver as biting air creepcrawls into my lungs. *Feels like it's getting colder by the minute*, Jopa says. *Ants don't like cold.* He tells me how they go into a state called diapause to survive. I nudge his shoulder. *Like the sleeping medicine Tiev gave you.* He quirkfaces. *I didn't know I was so much like an ant.* Somehow his delight in being like an ant helps me be more forgiving of what Jopa's family did.

When the supply truck rumbles in from a station near the Worselands–Wilds border, we watch robos unload boxes of memory cards and battery packs along with a whole row of military-issue caskets, ready to be filled. For so many, this is the end of their journey, the end of their life.

I lay my head against D-39's back and say a prayer for peace.

For Peace

The next day when Dr. Wesl gives D-39 her daily checkup, my heart doesn't snapcrackle with concern. It stays strong and confident like Papa's voice when he's talking about looganuts. I don't need Dr. Wesl's stethoscope to know my dog is better. *Thank you*, I say when he gives me the thumbs-up.

I take a deep breath. It's now or never. *I need to tell you something.* I finally share about Nuni, because I need the peace that comes from telling the truth. My insides will churn forever if I don't, and it's the right thing to do. Tears stream down his cheeks, and he doesn't try to hide them. *Thank you for telling me. She was—* He clears his throat. *Amazing*, I fill in. Even if she was for the government, she sent us to Dr. Wesl. He nods. *Yes.* His snickergiggle is gargly with tears. *Yes. Hey, Klynt, I've got something to tell you, too. It's time.*

Time

My wet eyes meet Dr. Wesl's. *I've arranged a transport for D-39. To get her safely to the Wilds.* My heart rammerjammers, and I am overcome with gratitude. *When do we leave?* His eyelids shutterbug. *Only D-39.*

I think I've heard him wrong. I must have heard him wrong. *But she's my dog. She goes where I go.* He shakes his head. *I'm sorry, but that's not how the K-9 Corridor works. The priority is and always has been to get the dogs out of the Worselands.*

My voice rises. *But* we're *on our way out of the Worselands! We don't need the K-9 Corridor. We're going to cross at the International Peace Garden, and we're taking D-39 with us.*

He places a hand on my arm. *Listen to me, Klynt. You can't bring a dog over the border like that. Especially at the Peace Garden crossing. That's one of the biggest refugee camps! And you can't know this, but time stops in places like that. If they catch her, they'll quarantine her as a precaution against BrkX. They can't have a sickness sweeping a refugee camp.*

Refugee Camp

I focus on Dr. Wesl's voice rather than how flipfurious I am that he would suggest we send D-39 off with some transport. Nuni apparently didn't know him as well as she thought. His betrayal is a kick in the gut. *The camp*, he says, *is thirty miles from here, on the Wilds side of the Peace Garden.* I nod. That's just a few miles from Everlake. And we visited the garden when I was in kinderschool, before the ongoing death-stretch made field trips impossible.

He explains that the camp is now more permanent than makeshift, and it's full to bursting. *It's like a town, with water and food and books and clothes. They even have a school and a hospital.* He blinks. *You and Jopa will be safe there. But if they see D-39, they will capture her immediately and keep her for weeks. You don't want that, do you?*

What a stupid question. Of course I don't want that. Nuni's words come to me again: *Trust no one.* Was she talking about Dr. Wesl, too? I can't be sure, so I play along. *No*, I say. *That's not what I want.* And it won't happen. Because I have a better idea.

Idea

I don't say it to Dr. Wesl, but I know what we will do. Jopa and I will put D-39 back in the casing. Make her look like a robo again. I grimace. I hate the thought of the plastic digging into her skin. But I hate the thought of being without my dog even more.

I've arranged a transport for you, too, Dr. Wesl says. *It's been great having you around, but now that you're better* . . . His words trail off, and his eyes get a little shiny. I think he truly has enjoyed having us at the supply camp.

Thank you, I sweetmurmur, though my stomach is still flutterbugged about him suggesting we separate from D-39. Dr. Wesl has done so much for us and for D-39. We might not be alive without him. But still. I take a step back from him and cross my arms against my chest so he won't try to upcuddle me. His face droopbottoms. *Be ready*, he says. *The vans will leave tonight.*

Tonight

When I tell Jopa about Dr. Wesl's plan to take D-39, he quiverquakes. *No way*, he says.

Together we prep D-39's decoy robo gear. It takes a few hours to first get the parts from the spare room, and then to fashion them into something believable. But as soon as I find the chestplate with the Dog Alive logo, I know I can make it work. *Dog Alive*, Jopa says. *That's funny*. I quirkface. D-39 will once again be a dog alive disguised as a Dog Alive.

With the help of my trusty screwdriver, five just-right screws that Jopa's ant-eyes spot in a dark corner, and a small blow-torch we find in Dr. Wesl's office, we make D-39 a whole new set of armor.

No way can I sleep knowing that a knock is coming tonight that will take us away from the deathstretch. I stroke D-39 ears-to-tail and sit up with Jopa, who has a thousand questions about the

Peace Garden refugee camp. *Other kids will be there? Our families will find us? We'll be free?*

Free. I touch my fingers to his lips. That word is so hopeful, so fragile that I don't like saying it out loud.

Out Loud

When the knock comes, I think of Papa, and wish it were him knocking. The air is frigid and smells of cold-dust, though none is falling. Yet.

Thanks to the dark and the hurryscurry, we are behind the supply station before Dr. Wesl notices D-39's robo disguise. His right brow jagsaws, then his eyes bigsky. *How did you—* he asks. *Why?* And then his face changes. He gets it. Lucky for us he cares too much about the mission of the K-9 Corridor to say anything else out loud that might reveal D-39. *Klynt. Don't do this. You'll be sorry.*

D-39 is mine. She stays with me. He shakes his head. *You're just like Nuni. You take too many risks.* He takes a big breath, and I hold tight to D-39, half expecting him to try to tear her away from me. But he doesn't.

As a van wheels in, Dr. Wesl's beeper goes off. He looks at his device. *It's the K-9 Corridor. I'll tell them we've had a change of plans.* After *you are on your way.* He pulls open the side door where the seats are already crammed with half a dozen strangers.

This is it, Dr. Wesl sweetmurmurs. *The van will take you to a drop-off site we've used successfully for the past month. You'll walk across from there. Good luck.* My heart thud-jams. He's letting us go. Nuni was right about him after all.

Thank you, I say to Dr. Wesl. *We'll never forget you*, Jopa says, and Dr. Wesl melts into the darkness.

When I call to D-39 to hop in, the driver shakes his head. *No one told me about a robo.* My hand tightens on D-39's shoulder-plate. *We're a package deal*, I say. The driver swears. *Then you'll have to wait for another transport.* He shifts in his seat as the techies adjust something in the engine under the van's front hood. *No robos. That's the rule.*

Rule

We can't wait, I tell Jopa. *This is our transport.* I grab his hand and we hurryscurry around to the open-top trailer that's attached to the back of the van. I don't care what the driver says. We're leaving now. Together. Even if it means riding in the trailer. We won't wait, and we won't be separated. It's too risky.

Are you listening, Mama? We're staying together. Even though the driver refused us and the trailer is filled with brand-new caskets. We follow our own rules. We will stay together.

Together

We have to get inside of one? Jopa asks. I quirkface. It's perfect. No one would ever think to look for us in a casket. *It's fine, Jopa. It's brilliant!* I look toward the van and see that the driver is now standing with the techie looking under the hood. I tip open the top and call D-39. *Up*, I command. She hops right in, tail jerkwagging like it's no big deal.

See? I tell Jopa. *D-39 likes it. It's got to be fine.* Jopa doesn't quite quirkface, but he ramscrambles inside, grumbling something about how D-39 also likes to lick the insides of cans, and we don't do that.

I'm next. I hear the techies click the van hood back into place, and I wigglesquirm in between Jopa and D-39. It's a tight fit in there together, but not unbearable. Once we're all settled, I use the edge of my map to just crack the top. Not enough to be noticed, but enough to let in some air. Within seconds that casket is bursting with life. The van engine gives a low whine, and we're on our way.

Our Way

We lie in the casket for what feels like hours. My arms are across Jopa's back, his feet across my shins. Every time we think the van must be stopping, its engine roars us forward. I'm not sure we will ever get there.

D-39 keeps us warm, her sweet breath filling the small space. I finger her scratch-patched ear and lean my face against her chestplate. Her decoy motor hums steady as ever. If I didn't know there was a real dog under all that metal, I'd never guess it. Obviously.

Every part of me aches, and still somehow I sleep.

Sleep

It feels like hours pass before the van finally stops. *Is it over?* Jopa says. *Or am I still asleep?* He starts to push his way out. *Wait*, I say and hardpress him back down. The van's brought us as close as it dares. *The rest of the way we must walk.*

We hear the door creak open and the crunch of boots on the ground as the people pour out. They're quiet, all things considered. They have to be—*we* have to be—because crossing this border is illegal. Anyone who gets caught goes back to the Worselands if they have enough currency to pay the fines. Otherwise they're sent to government work camps. *Now*, I say, praying it's safe. Making myself trust and moving forward.

Forward

Nobody sees us clamber out of the casket.
As we creepcrawl behind a group of three,
I realize it's every person for themselves
now. Best to space out until we get across
officially. My stomach fistclenches, and my
neck feels tight enough to snap. I want us
to be across, where it's safe.

We follow from a distance until we're alone,
and the hair on the back of my neck lifts. I
grip Jopa's hand and hold on to D-39's collar
as I scan the perimeter. *Are we there yet?*
asks Jopa. I release his hand. *I'm not sure.*
I'd hoped everything would look different
so we'd know. But these woods look just
like the woods in the Worselands. As if
we're still in the bush.

I jump when bellsong tinkles through the
leafgiants. To the far left and just behind
us, a guard tower rises above the treeline.
Stone-walled, like they showed on the
streamscreen so long ago. My stomach
swarms with flutterbugs. We've passed the
tower. We're actually past it. *Jopa.* I grab
his cheeks, and D-39 prancedances around
us. *We made it! We made it to the Wilds!*

The Wilds

Jopa's voice quiverquakes, and a brisk blusterblow lifts the hair from his forehead.
It doesn't feel real. I point out the white
tops of the tents and trailers. *See, Jopa?* It
looks like a refugee camp to me. *We're safe.*
I upcuddle D-39's neck. *We're safe, D-39.*
And we're so close to Everlake—our new
home—where we can live and play and be
without fear.

Without Fear

Trouble is, after being cooped up in the casket for so long, D-39 wants to play now. She's feeling better, so her tail plumes high and she nips at my fingers, begging me to play chase or fetch or anything. I can't deny her, so when we come to a pond, I set down my pack. *Let's stop here for a few minutes. What do you say?*

Jopa pumps his fist. He lifts a stick from the ground. *I'll throw it for her,* he volunteers. D-39 flies after it like she was never sick. She splashes around the shore, getting all four paws wet, like it's not even freeze-season. As if it's just another day. How lucky to be a dog, to live in the moment without human worries.

I take a deep breath, joyslammed for a jinglesnap that we aren't cramped in a casket and there are no dead things in the water, bloated and floating. I'd forgotten what it was like to exist without fear. And that's when I hear it. Mama's voice: *Now, Klynt. The time is now.*

Now

I know we should get moving, but when D-39 comes out of the water her chestplate flashes an error. *Beep, beep, beep!* When she shakes the bluewater from her fur, the signal gets louder. It's so loud that even D-39 starts to whine. *It's okay*, I soothe and start pushing buttons.

Nothing works. The signal only gets louder. D-39 turns in a circle, barking. She wants the noise to stop right now. *Okay, okay.* I grab her collar and bang on the chestplate with my fist. When I hold my palm against it, the beeping stops. But soon as I lift my palm, the noise begins again. Hey hi ho there. How am I supposed to keep the button pressed and walk at the same time? It just isn't possible.

Possible

We're going to have to strip the metal, I announce. Even though it sends a quiver-quake down my spine after what Dr. Wesl said about the refugee camp's canine quarantine policy. They'll pick her up, unless they think she's a robo.

Beep, beep, beep! I don't want to put D-39 in danger, but what else can I do? I've got to believe the saying Papa taught me to believe. Anything is possible. *Follow me*, I tell Jopa. We've got to hike deeper in the woods so I can fix D-39.

Fix D-39

We retreat to the privacy of a pine glen, and I peel away D-39's casing. Right away the beeping stops, and D-39 stops barking. *She's hurt*, Jopa says, pointing to her shoulders. She's got new sores, rawfire and bleeding. I pat her head. *I'm sorry, girl.* I must have made it too tight or crafted it wrong. There just wasn't enough time. I study her abrasions and stroke her silky ears. I know the casing is the reason she's alive. But no way can I case her back up. Not now.

Jopa, let's rest for a while. Give D-39 a little time without the shell. Then we'll try again. Jopa quirkfaces. Like now that he knows we're safely in the Wilds, he needs a break, too. I guess we all do. He pulls out his ant jar and uses the base of the slingshot like a trowel, digging in the loamy dirt. *That'll give me time to hunt for some ants.*

Ants

I watch Jopa for a few minutes, but my eyelids are heavy. I must rest them.

I dream of ants. It's a long dream, in which I am walking and walking, never getting anywhere. Probably the way an ant feels on any given day.

I startle awake when a low-in-the-throat bark cuts the air. *D-39?* I ramscramble to my feet. *What?* Jopa says. *What's happening?*

Not ten yards away, two tall figures move through the leafgiants, all dark shadows. The air is so cold that I can see my breath. We've slept away the afternoon and now my animal body is screaming, *Danger!*

Danger

Hey! I shout when I see a flash of D-39's golden fur. But I'm too late. The figures muzzle and leash her. *Stop! That's my dog!* I hurryscurry toward them, Jopa's hand tucked in mine. The men shrug. *Sorry kid,* the taller one says. *It's the law.*

No. My breath whifflegusts and my heart thudjams so violently I have to hardpress my hand against my chest. *Please. She doesn't have BrkX, I promise.*

She could be a carrier, the tall one says, leading D-39 to the back of a souped-up ATV with a stack of two dog crates. *But she's not,* I tell them. *We have to be sure,* he says. I watch helplessly as they place D-39 inside, and the door clanks shut behind her.

It's just like Dr. Wesl warned. I press my hand against the wire, and D-39 can't even lick me because of the muzzle. She whines, and I nearly collapse. *Where are you taking her?* Jopa asks. *How do we get her back?*

If the men respond, I don't hear them.
That's how loud my heartbeat is in my ears.
As the ATV wheels away, I see paint on the
side that reads, "Animal Control."

Animal Control

Stop! I say again as engine fumes tickle my nose. I fall to my knees. *Oh, Jopa. We were so close. So close.* I still can't believe they took D-39. I saw it happen, and it doesn't feel real.

As the ATV is swallowed by the leafgiants, I still can't believe it. My dog—D-39—is gone. *Jopa, we have to follow that ATV. We have to get her back.* All this time I thought everything in the Wilds was free. Of course it's not. Is anything ever all the way free?

We will, K-K. We'll get her back for sure. Tears choke my throat. *Why, oh why did I take off her casing?* Jopa squeezes my hand. *You had to. Because of the beeping.* My head hangs. *But I shouldn't have fallen asleep.* I meet his eyes. *How could I have fallen asleep?*

Because you're a human, Jopa insists. *Not a robo.*

Not a Robo

I half quirkface. At least I always have Jopa. Sweetsavage, ant-loving Jopa. *We'll just explain it to them, right? That D-39 is my dog, and she's healthy. They'll do their tests, and they'll know she's not a threat to anyone.* I pick up the top half of D-39's casing. It's bulky and heavy. No way will we be able to lug it around. *We'll convince them to give her back to me. And once we leave the camp, we won't have to pretend anymore.*

Jopa's stomach rumbles so loud we both snickergiggle. *Maybe,* he says, *we should eat first.*

First

We jerkjolt into the camp past a maroon
flag that proves that we are officially in
another country. My first time out of the
Worselands. I don't see the ATV that took
D-39, but in different tents we find a mul-
titude of welcoming faces. They offer us
blankets and food, and we see a school, a
store, lights, plumbing. Just like Dr. Wesl
promised. All they ask in return is that we
first answer their questions.

Questions

When I tell them we have family waiting, they want to know names and addresses. A man with a kind face beckons us toward the door. *Won't you come inside? You and your brother will be warm, and you can fill out some forms.*

I don't tell him Jopa isn't my brother. Right now I feel like he is.

When the man quirkfaces, my insides fistclench. His questions, his kindness—it's too much. I don't want to be on his records. I only want to get D-39. So I grab my stomach and hunch. *Where is the poop-flush? It's an emergency.*

Emergency

The man escorts us down the hallway. *We can complete the forms when we get back*, he promises. We push through a corridor, past a cafeteria where people are loading their plates. As rich, delicious scents find our noses, Jopa backsteps to the cafeteria. *Can't we stay here? Look at all that food!* A hot bar holds steaming platters of meat and vegetables. There's also a fruit bar and sweets station. *They have chocolate nubs*, Jopa says, and rubs his hands together in anticipation. I can't help it: I upcuddle him. Chocolate is an emergency when you're six and your name is Jopa and you've missed some meals. *First we use the poopflush*, I tell him. *Deal?*

Deal

As our escort waits in the hallway, I search the restroom. Finally in the last stall I find it—a window. *Come on,* I tell Jopa as I lift the glass and a blast of cold air hits my face. *Let's go rescue D-39!* Because if we go back out to the escort, to the cafeteria, we'll be stuck. And who knows what will become of D-39?

With a little encouragement from me, Jopa ramscrambles up and out, and I follow. It isn't until we're shivering in the darkness that he remembers the cafeteria. *What about our deal?* he asks. *When are we going to go back and get something to eat?* I cringe. *I don't know,* I admit. *Let's find D-39, and then we'll figure it out.* Jopa crosses his arms against his chest but doesn't fuss. He wants to find D-39, too.

We check all the parking lots but can't find the ATV anywhere. I place my hands on my head and turn in a slow circle looking out, out, out. I see only emptiness. *Oh, D-39, where are you?*

Maybe, Jopa says, *the refugee workers are like ants. Ants want to keep their food clean, so they put their seed room far away from their trash room.*

Yes, Jopa! Why didn't I think of that? They probably put the dogs in some sort of outerbuilding. That's the deal with a quarantine, isn't it? Keep the risky ones away from the rest? We spy three metal buildings, all on the outskirts of the camp. *Listen*, I say. *Maybe we'll hear them.*

At first all I can hear is the noise coming from the dining hall, but then a bark enters my brain. Then more barks, yips, and squeals. *There!* I point to the shed farthest from the dining hall. I squeeze Jopa's shoulders. *Jopa, you're a genius.* He shrugs. *It's the ants.*

We run toward the shed, which isn't much more than a lean-to. I hate to think of D-39 in there. She must be so confused! It doesn't help that a guard stands just outside the door of the building. Jopa tugs my hand. *How are we going to get in?* My heart rammerjammers as an idea comes to my brain. *Jopa, how do you feel about being a distraction?*

Distraction

After we've talked it through, I'm still not sure Jopa all the way understands what he must do. But before I have a chance to ask him to repeat what I said, he takes off whining and dripfacing. I crouch low to watch and to pray. *Please, oh please, oh please let this work!* My chest is so tight I can barely breathe. It's all part of the plan.

The Plan

Jopa dripfaces so convincingly that I am not zapjawed when the guard takes his hand and starts walking him toward the tent city. That was the plan: for Jopa to get rid of the guard by saying he's lost. Who wouldn't want to help a cute kid like him?

As soon as they have turned the corner I hurryscurry toward the Animal Control door and turn the handle. Locked. Of course. I twist again. The door doesn't budge. That's when I remember what's in my pocket, like always.

Always

I use my screwdriver to try to pry the knob from the door, but it's one solid piece of metal instead of the two-piece model I was hoping for.

Next I try sliding the driver above the knob into the narrow space where the door meets the door frame. My fingers are stiff with cold, and the screwdriver keeps slipping. *Come on*, I urge, hoping to activate the tongue of the lock. I jiggle and hardpress, but it still won't catch.

The volume of barking from inside increases, and I'm sure the dogs can hear me scratching around. Does D-39 know we're coming for her? That no matter what, I will always come for her? Can she smell me outside this door? Thoughts of her in there waiting for me renew my commitment. I can't stop just because it's hard. I have to keep at it until it works.

I hardpress and jiggle some more, and just when I think my fingers are too cramped to do any more, the screwdriver catches the tongue. When I grasp the knob, the door eases open.

My whole body quiverquakes from cold and anticipation as I push open the door. The dogs feed off my energy, and the cacophony is deafening. It's like I have discovered Planet Dog.

Planet Dog

I can't believe how many dogs there are in such a small space. The shed is no bigger than our barn at the Anchor T. One wall is lined top to bottom with crates. Largest dogs are on the bottom and smaller ones up top. I peek in at all their faces as I walk past.

Where is she? Where is she?

My chest feels like a tank is parked on top of me as I get to the end of the row. She's not in the building. D-39 is not here.

Not Here

I barge through the back door of the shed without stopping. Are we in the wrong place? Is it possible I'm too late? What if they transported her to another shelter? What if she's not here because one of the Animal Control people fell in love with her and took her home? It could totally happen. I know, because that's what I did.

But no. It's only been an hour, maybe two, since Animal Control picked her up. D-39 has to be here. Somewhere in this camp. But where?

Tears prick my eyes. I don't even care now if I get caught. I must find D-39. If I have to check every single room of every single structure in this camp, I'll do it.

I push the next door open. It's an office building of some sort with a long corridor and doors along either side. I race down the hall, throwing open doors as I pass. I call my dog. *D-39! D-39!*

People look up from desks. One woman in a lab coat drops her coffee mug. A man in a uniform centers himself in the hallway to block my passage. He expects me to stop, but I don't. I'm like an upstart tornado. I bear down even harder.

Even Harder

I hardpress into him, whipwhirling as I go. For a second he catches me, but I make myself slipsloppy. I realquick drop down to the concrete floor and slide between his legs.

As he curses, I keep going. *D-39!* I shout. More whitecoats. Tiny medical rooms with exam tables, some of them occupied by humans. When a flash of gold catches my eye, I'm sure it's D-39.

But it isn't. It's a bouncy kid about Jopa's size in a gold-colored shirt. My heart sinks. This can't all be for nothing. D-39 has to be here somewhere.

I'm cruising toward the rear exit door when I hear a familiar sound above the din. *Arf, arf, arf!* I know it's her. *D-39!* I call, and sure enough, she replies. *Arf. Arf. Arf.* I follow the sound and turn into the last room on the hallway. And there she is, in a crate beside two other dogs. *D-39!* My fingers are lightning fast as I unlatch the gate. She licks my face as I throw my arms around her neck, squeezing even harder than ever before.

Once D-39 saved me. This time I'm saving her. But not by myself. *We* are saving her. K-K and Jopa to the rescue!

Rescue

I pull D-39 toward the door. *Wait!* one of
the whitecoats shouts. But I don't wait.
Adrenaline courses through me. I've got my
dog, and nothing will stop me now. I keep
my hand on D-39's shoulder as we race out
of the building into the bright unknown.

The Bright Unknown

We're not more than fifty yards from the building when I hear shouts and a siren. They're after us, as I suspected they would be. They can't allow a possibly infected dog loose. I get that. But she's not infected. She's not.

Please let Jopa be where we planned—in our hiding spot in the woods. We can't enjoy any refugee-camp comforts, not when they'll want to reclaim D-39. We just have to get through the night. And then it will be morning. We'll be better rested, in much better condition for our last trek—to Everlake. We'll keep moving until we get there.

Are you there, Mama? Can you hear me? We're so close. Like magic, her voice comes to me: *Follow the blue paint.* I look up at the leafgiants, but it's too dark to see if any of them are marked with blue paintslashes. I hurry into the hollow, and there he is. *Jopa!* In his arms he holds a bundle. A coat, socks, scarf, and hat. Gifts from the refugee center. *You did so good!*

Jopa snickergiggles as D-39 licks his face all over. *I knew it would work,* he says. *Tomorrow,* I tell Jopa. *Tomorrow we'll find the trail.*

The Trail

We sleep in an evergreen thicket with our
bellies hard balls of hunger. If only we'd
had time to feast in that cafeteria! Even
with every inch of our skin covered, somehow the cold still seeps in. D-39 is the first
to wake. I lipbrush her right between the
eyes. *Jopa*, I say. *Are you awake?* He pushes
the hood of the coat back and all I see are
his bigsky eyes. *I guess that's a yes*. He
quirkfaces, and we gather our things and
start walking. We need as much of a head
start as we can get in case anyone decides
to continue the search for D-39.

We've been walking less than an hour
when Jopa spots blue paintslashes high
on the leafgiants. *That's our map, right?*
The marks are subtle, nothing fancy at all.
They're so high up you probably wouldn't
notice them unless you knew to look.
How'd they do that? I shrug, because I don't
know. *We'll have to ask them*. It's one of the
things I wish I could ask Papa. He's the
one who told me about the blue paint in
the first place, almost as if he knew that

someday I'd be here doing this. The paint was Mama's idea, a secret code of sorts, for volunteers delivering dogs along the K-9 Corridor.

Are we close, K-K? Jopa's voice is small and puddleglum. No one—not even Jopa—wants to get there more than I do. *Come on*, I coax. *It's not that far.*

Far

D-39 scouts ahead of us. She comes and goes, always checking back, never going too far ahead. *The best way to journey*, I tell Jopa, *is to rest every two hours.* My voice sounds like Papa. *Walk, don't run. Steady, steady. More faithful sun than fickle moon.* Jopa doesn't respond, just keeps going, trudging along. *Hey*, I suggest, *why don't you sing an antsong?*

Antsong

The tune is slow, puddleglum. *Queen ant lays eggs all day, eggs all day, eggs all day. Queen ant lays eggs all day. All hail the queen.*

If any of us is queen, it's D-39. I'm just glad that this time we're not dragging her along on a bedsheet. Today, thank goodness, she pads beside us, all on her own. She pants and every so often bumps my leg with her nose.

Once she even steals my glove. *D-39, no,* I scold. I expect Jopa to snickergiggle or at least quirkface at her antics. Instead, his song fades to silence.

Silence

Jopa stumbles on a root and falls to the ground, says he can't take another step. *We should have stayed at the refugee camp.* It's so quiet I can hear myself swallow. How can I convince him this is all going to be worth it? That Everlake will be better than chocolate nubs? *I know you're tired, Jopa. I am, too.* It hasn't been two hours yet, but sometimes plans must change. *Want to rest for a little while? Then go again?*

Right away he nods. Neither of us has the energy to collect wood for a fire, so we huddle together against the cold-getting-colder air. We're so close that a strand of Jopa's hair gets caught in my mouth. Eventually D-39 settles beside us. I lie awake listening to both her and Jopa's breathing.

The sky goes on forever. How strange that when we were in the burrow, I longed for sky. And now all I want is a blanket and a roof. Soon, I think. Soon. I let my eyelids close. We sleep this way until late afternoon.

Afternoon

A raven swoops overhead, and its wings are writing in cursive against the parchment sky. I think of Papa. He would know what a raven's visit might mean for the weather, the Anchor T, the looganut fields.

Mama's voice comes to me: *Keep going.* D-39 snuffles. Jopa sighs. And when I look up, I see that where the raven was, now drifting down like tiny secret messages are cold-dustflakes.

Cold-Dustflakes

We trudge forward, following the blue paintslashes. By dusk all the woods are frosted in two inches of white. All D-39 wants to do is plunder, digging into it with her nose for what might be hidden underneath. *Hurry*, I tell Jopa, forgetting about steadysteady or any of Papa's rules. The last thing we want is to be in these woods when the cold-dust piles up. Our steps will be slower, and the moisture will soak through our shoes and pantlegs.

I remember back at the Anchor T how it seemed to me that cold-dust erased the world. But now I know it also magnifies everything. Our breath, our footprints. The distance between paintslashes. The deathripped world, so big and messy and complicated. My hollowed-out heart is desperate for the end of something, or the beginning, or I don't know what.

We must get to Everlake because I'm not sure we have enough strength to survive even one cold-duststorm in the Wilds during freezeseason.

Freezeseason

The deepening layer of cold-dust means new dangers and discomforts: ice-block feet and no more knowing if there's a hole to dodge. How will we build a fire? I clamp my jaw and reach for the canteen Nuni gave us, but it's not there. I pat all around, my heart like a jumping bean. *Jopa? Do you have the canteen?* D-39's eyes follow my every movement. She paces, whines. Jopa's eyes turn dark and liquid as he shakes his head. *It's lost.*

Lost

I brush cold-dust off a log and sit down, D-39's head on my knee. How could we have lost the canteen? I hardpress my fingers against my temples, hoping that will help me remember the last time we drank from it. Where were we? What were we doing? But even if I could remember, it doesn't matter. The canteen is gone. I have to accept it.

As Jopa settles in beside me, I make myself switch gears. *We can melt cold-dust with our hands*, I say, and Jopa's face brightens briefly. I don't tell him that cold-dust is mostly air, which means it takes quite a lot of it to get much water. Instead I use the time to tell Jopa another story—this one about a colony of ants who befriend a lost boy. When the boy brings them water, they name him Ant King. *I wonder how the queen feels about that*, Jopa says. I squeeze him close to me. It's reassuring to know he hasn't lost his sense of humor.

As he snuggles into my side, he tells me that ants can't see all that well. They communicate by smell. *That's their best trick,* Jopa says. *That's how they show each other the way.*

The Way

I close my eyes and listen for Mama's voice.
I think back over my restoration projects
and everything Papa taught me. Nothing
comes to me. No advice, no words of
wisdom. I lipbrush D-39's nose. *What now,
D-39?* She looks around, ears perked, nose
quiverquaking. Waiting for me—trusting
me—to move first so she can follow.

As flutterbugs invade my stomach, my
mind turns clear as the river before the
deathstretch. We must keep going. Keep
following the blue paintslashes. It can't be
much farther. It can't be. *Everlake is that
way.* I point with confidence. *They'll give
us water. If we hurry, we can even get there
by nightfall.*

Nightfall

As the first stars pop out, my legs are so heavy they feel disconnected from my body. *We should stop again*, Jopa says. I know he's right, but we're so close. We have to be.

Just a little farther, I promise. He shakes his head. *No. I'm too tired.* I squat next to him. *Hey*, I say. *I know it's been a long day. Pretend you're Tiev. She wouldn't stop, would she?*

I am not *Tiev*, he counters. *I wish we had a sled. Like Jonah in* The Giver. I turn to D-39. *A sled would be nice, wouldn't it?* D-39 licks my hand. Then her head jerks as a branch snaps. I don't even have time to draw my screwdriver when I see it: a moose.

Moose

Not just one moose—it's three. A square-faced mama with two fuzzy brown yearlings. I lift my arms to encircle D-39, to keep her from chasing them. But I'm too late. She bounds toward the mama moose like it's a long-lost friend. When the moose pins back her ears and lowers her head, I know exactly what's happening—we're under attack.

Attack

D-39, I shout. *No!* But it's too late. The year-lings grunt as the mama moose charges toward us, so fast there isn't time to run. I wave my arms, shout, but the moose's hooves pound the earth, sending cold-dust flying. *Go away!* I shout. But the mama moose doesn't go away.

Away

Behind me Jopa whips something out of our pack. I hear it before I see it: The brush of fabric against air. It's the rainbow sky-sail, swaying in Jopa's small hands. *STOP!*

The moose swerves, wheels away as the skysail's colorful tail splashes against waves of white.

Waves of White

When I can breathe again, I grab Jopa's shoulders. *You saved us.* He shrugs. *The skysail did.* I bury my face against D-39's neckfur, stroke her ears. *You jayballs dog. Don't you know you can't make friends with a moose?* D-39 whines, like she's telling me she didn't know and asking why I didn't mention it sooner. Jopa and I both snicker-giggle at her antics, and the adrenaline makes me feel strong. *Jopa, what if I carry you? You can be the captain, and I'll be your ship cruising this white-wave sea.* His eyes brighten, and my chest expands with hope. I turn around so he can climb aboard my back as fresh cold-dust begins to form drifts between the leafgiants.

Between the Leafgiants

I wonder if the white world will swallow us before we ever make it. My legs move, but I don't feel them. I am less human, more machine. I am turning robo.

When I hear a twig snap, I jolt and grab hold of D-39's collar. I instantly imagine another moose or someone from the camp come to collect my dog. Or something even more threatening: a desperado with a gun. My heart jerkthumps as I scan for boots, ATV tracks, or wolf or moose prints.

But it isn't anything like that. It's just a girl—probably no more than a year or two older than I am, draped in a thickneck shawl. She reaches her hand out to me. *Welcome to Everlake.*

VIII.

Everlake

I gulp. We made it. We really made it. I want to quirkface, but I'm too zapjawed. Can it really be? After our long, crooked journey, and all my years of yearning?

My tongue is frozen. My feet are as cold-stiff as wood, my cheeks blusterblow-chapped, my belly a cavern. We've stepped inside my forever-dream, and now I'm drowning at the sight of a girl in a thickneck shawl—a girl from Everlake. I upcuddle both D-39 and Jopa. Only then do I accept the girl's hand and offer a greeting.

Greeting

The girl kneels to scratch D-39 behind the ears, and my dog rolls over so the girl can rub her belly. A thick ginger braid hangs over one of her shoulders, and her strawberry freckles make constellations on her cheeks and nose. She's our north star, and we follow her through the leafgiants into a clearing that becomes a path lined with plain cinder-block buildings. My insides fold in on themselves and drop down, down as we pass doors painted sunsplash colors and strung with twinklelights. Is this place really real? The sky glows red—a reminder that somewhere, something or someone is burning.

Burning

I have a million questions I want to ask, but the first is most important: *My name is Klynt Tovis. I'm looking for my mother, Ersu Tovis. Do you know her?*

Her

The girl stares at me hard. *You're Klynt?* At the sound of my name, D-39's tail swish-swipes. When I nod, the girl grabs my chin, tilting my face from side to side.

Your dimple. She quirkfaces, as if I've passed inspection. *It's just like hers.* Her cheeks turn rosy, and her freckles darken. *You* are *Klynt!* Then she focuses on Jopa. *And who are you?*

Jopa rubs his eyes. *Jopa Jax Tannin. I'm tired. And hungry. Klynt made us hurry all day.* I throw an arm around him, and the girl's lips turn into a perfect bow as she reassures him that we'll soon have food and shelter. She links her arm with mine. *I told Mama you'd come.* Her eyes glimmer-spark. *I told her we'd be sisters.*

Sisters

I untangle my arm from hers. *Sisters?* The girl quirkfaces. *Not blood sisters, obviously.* I think she means because we look like opposites—me all dark, her all light. *My name's Zion. I've lived here for five years now, ever since—* Her eyes droopbottom in a way that I instantly understand. Something bad happened. So bad that she won't—or can't—talk about it. *That's when Mama took me in.* Her face brightens again. *And now you're here. So we can be sisters for real!*

For Real

Zion calls Mama *Mama,* too? I have a sister?

My heart stops. Completely, utterly stops.
How is this happening? Mama not only left
me, she *replaced* me.

No wonder she never came back to the
Anchor T. It wasn't only about the dogs.
She had this girl who needed her. This
living, breathing human named Zion. Heat
creepcrawls out from the center of my
chest and fills my whole body. Mama went
and got herself a whole new daughter!

I call D-39 to my side. Zion may be my
mother's daughter, but she is not my sister.
Where is she? I ask. *Where is my mother?*

Mother

This way, Zion says. *Mama should be done with rounds and back at our unit by now.* We follow her to the end of a side street to a halfdug in a hillside. *For energy efficiency*, she says. The door is painted red. Just red. No flowers or twinklelights.

Zion's steps are light, excited, while mine feel like I am hauling bricks on my back. I keep my hand tucked in D-39's neckfur, and it steadies me.

And then the door is creaking open, light spilling into the darkening street. Two dogs greet us: one with a docked tail that Zion calls East and the other twice the size of D-39 that she calls West. The dogs sniff and circle each other, making their own introductions. And then I see her. My mother.

Mama's hair is dark like mine, her nose tilted up like mine. And yes, there's the dimple. The dimple from the photograph. *My* dimple. She's tall and commanding, as if certain of her place in the world. Of course the dogs love her. She's so obviously the leader of the pack.

Zion dances around us, like she's brought Mama the best surprise. *Can you believe it, Mama? Klynt found us, just like you always said she would.* Mama examines me with her calm, steady gaze. *You're really here,* she says, her eyes not leaving mine. *Please. Come in out of the cold.*

Cold

Mama. My mama. Here. And me full of not-knowing: How do you greet a mother you don't remember? How do you say hello to a hero? My whole body quiverquakes. I don't know if I should upcuddle her or lip-brush her or what. It doesn't help that she stands there, cold, as if we are strangers. Because we *are* strangers.

Strangers

My hand settles onto the smooth, reliable handle of my screwdriver in my pocket. My mind blizzards, and all my thoughts are hazy and confused.

Why isn't she upcuddling me? She isn't acting like a mother. She doesn't even seem particularly glad to see me. But then, why would she be glad, when she's had Zion all this time? I'm a stranger. And not only that, she doesn't sound right. Her voice is all wrong.

With one hand I grip D-39, and with the other I yank out the screwdriver, point it at her face. *Tell me the truth.* All *of it.*

All of It

Jopa gasps. *K-K! Stop!* But I can't. I have to know. The woman who says she is my mother lifts her hands in surrender. *Okay, okay. Settle down. You've had a long journey, and this must be a shock.* She reaches for a frame on the mantel. *I promise I'll tell you everything—all of it. But first, let's start with this photograph.*

Photograph

She hands me a worn picture that shows a younger version of her with a younger version of Papa holding baby me in front of the barn. The good old barn where I first found D-39, the barn that is no more. I can see the looganut fields all around.

Their faces are smooth and quirkfacing, while my face is barely visible, thanks to me being so small, and because my head is turned away from the camera. A couple of cows and a horse graze in the background, and sitting in the grass between my parents is a black-and-white puppy. *Is that a robo?* I ask, even though I am pretty sure it's not. She quirkfaces. *That was the first one—the first dog we saved.* She returns the photo to the mantel and holds out her hand for me to shake. *You can call me Ersu.*

Ersu

I can't catch my breath. I can't believe the mama I knew—the mama I imagined—doesn't exist. What exists is Ersu.

I tear away from them, D-39 loping at my side. Jopa screams, *K-K, wait!* But I can't. I keep running until I come to a knoll where rows of painted boulders mark what can only be endstops.

I read their names: Ruby, Scout, Sasha, Buster. Dogs, not people. My mother, not my mother. The voice in my head all my life, not Mama's. Just something I made up. All this time, I've been listening to a ghost.

Ghost

I swallow. My whole body prickletwitches.
I still can't believe it. Part of me wishes
she were dead the way Papa said.

When Jopa finds me, he punches my arm.
I said, wait. I throw an arm around his
shoulders. *I know. I'm sorry.* I hardpress
my face against D-39's neck, but it doesn't
help. My stomach heaves, and I chugspew.

All this time I thought it was Papa's stub-
bornness keeping our family split apart.
His attachment to the Worselands and the
looganuts and the Anchor T. I thought
maybe Mama felt forgotten, unimportant,
the invisible-ghost way I've felt before.
That somehow Papa had made her feel
unwelcome.

I was wrong. Who knows what else I am
wrong about? I wipe my mouth. *Jopa, I'm
so sorry. This isn't turning out at all the way
I expected.* Sure, we're safe. But part of me
feels like we came all this way for nothing.
What a waste.

Waste

It's Ersu who comes for us. If she notices my swollen eyes, she doesn't mention it. And I don't mention it, either. I won't waste any more words on her.

Come around here, she says. *There's something I want to show you.* We walk back past the halfdug, through a fenced yard with a sidewalk leading to a cinder-block building. As we enter, I resist the urge to cover my ears. Inside it's like the Animal Control building at the refugee camp, except no crates. All open space, dogs together. Black ones, tall ones, skinny ones, spotted ones.

Wow, Jopa says, giving voice to what I'm feeling but won't dare express. The dogs greet Ersu with wet noses and waving tails. D-39 joins the fray with a series of barks and whines, her tail jerkwagging like jayballs. *Most of these dogs are from the Worselands*, Ersu says. *Or they are descendants of those dogs.* Her face is shiny with pride.

These are the dogs she helped save. I should
be impressed. I should be proud, too. But all
I can think is: Me. What about me?

About Me

My chest feels like the time the printing press collapsed with me under it, and my head is a boomblast ready to explode. I can't take the noise of the dogs another minute. *But Papa said—* I clamp my mouth shut because Ersu isn't listening. She's sweettalking a huge brown dog.

My throat feels scratchy. Papa told me she was dead. She's not dead. She's also not the mama I thought she'd be. I can't let her see me dripface. Because I get it now. I understand why Papa decided to lie.

Lie

It seems so stupid now. This woman, my mother, Ersu, she may be a hero to dogs, but she's nothing to me. Nothing.

Papa told me the lie about Mama being killed in border crossfire because he wanted to protect me. Because he knew that the truth—*this* truth—would hurt me. Because that's what a papa does: soil-nurtures and prepares and teaches and listens.

He knew she was never coming back, would never leave this place, this life. Not for me or Papa or anyone. All this time I was the one lying. To myself.

Maybe Ersu loves me. I ball my fists. Maybe. But she loves the dogs—and Zion, I think—more. This is her life.

Life

By the time we get back to the house Ersu shares with Zion and the dogs, I am numb. It's not from the cold. Ersu and Zion are so easy with each other, the way I am with Jopa and D-39. The way I am with Papa.

Papa.

Does he know about Zion? Did he protect me from that knowledge, too? Longing and regret flood my heart. I should have been nicer to him. I could have listened more, tried to understand. But I didn't.

And now? Now who knows where he is. Those are times we'll never get back. And who knows what life is waiting for us after all that's happened? What if I never get a chance to tell him about this moment? I feel nothing for this woman. I watch Ersu swinging her arms, patting D-39, and I want there to be some surge in my heart, some connection, but there's not.

Either I really am turning robo with no capacity for emotional connection, or she is. Or both.

Both

While Jopa chatters to Ersu and Zion, I am quiet. I wonder if this is what it feels like to be a robo. There, but not there.

Even with both D-39 and Jopa tucked close beside me that night, I hardly sleep. Same the next. When I finally do sleep, I don't wake for two days.

I didn't know if you would ever wake up, Jopa says. Beside him D-39's tail does more than jerkwag. It helicopters. *I'm glad to see you, too*, I say, and nuzzle her nose with mine.

Zion offers biscuits with homemade blueberry jam. Ersu quirkfaces to see me awake but doesn't linger. *Be back after I feed the dogs*, she announces as she slowly pulls the door shut.

Shut

As the days pass and the cold sharpens
and deepens, we spend most of our time
tucked inside the halfdug with the plain
red door. Four humans, three dogs, and a
jar that wants ants.

My mind hurricanes with thoughts about
Papa. I remember the look on his face when
he left for rations day, right before he shut
the hatch. When he said he would come
back. How he must have felt when he came
back and we weren't there, but maybe the
lion-man was.

I shake my head. I can't think about that. I
can't. What if I never see him again? What
if— What if I never get the chance to tell
him that I know the truth about Mama,
and I'm sorry?

Sorry?

Each day I help Ersu and Zion feed the dogs and sparkshine the kennel. They know names and ailments and personalities without looking at any charts.

Ersu quirkfaces and cuddles the dogs. Zion is her shadow, and East and West are always there. Watching them, I'm sorry I'm not a dog. Sorry I don't really fit well into this picture.

This Picture

By the time freezeseason solstice arrives, we've been at Everlake for a few weeks. Everyone leashes a dog or two and gathers to celebrate the shortest day, which marks the coming of longer ones, along with the return of light.

The just-frozen lake sparkles like sugar toast. Ersu and others dance by a bonfire while drummers drum. Here it doesn't matter if there is smoke or if the dogs howl and bark.

We are safe. I breathe deep for the first time in what feels like months. When D-39 sneaks up beside me and snags my glove, I quirkface fast and long. I clutch the screwdriver in my pocket whenever I think of Papa—where he might be and what's happening to him.

A voice rises over the singing and the instruments. It's the same voice I've heard so many times before. The voice I thought was Mama's, but isn't. *Wait, Klynt. And he will come.* So here I am, waiting for Papa.

For Papa

The days lengthen, but freezeseason drags. I get so humdrummed of the halfdug house and watching Ersu snuggle up with East and West. It's all I can do to keep from screaming.

But I don't scream, because Papa never screamed about Mama. Not once. It helps if I pretend Ersu's a new friend, rather than my mother. Zion's happy chatter eases everything, and part of me wishes we really were sisters. She cooks flatcakes for Jopa and me in the morning and tells us stories at night. Every one of them is about horses or sheep or dogs, not about what happened to her and how she ended up with Mama.

I dream of Papa, of the Anchor T the way it used to be, and of my once-upon-a-time Museum of Fond Memories. I marvel over how things change and don't change.

Change

When freezeseason breaks and the cold-
dust begins to melt, we go to Everlake's
community school, where everyone teaches
a class about something they know. I learn
to identify leafgiants, and I sketch faces.
We do pottery and whittling. *Soon it will
be your turn to teach a class*, Ersu says.
Right away Jopa decides his class will be
about ants. *You can do survival stuff, Klynt.
Or all about your museum*, he says. I stroke
D-39's head. Yes, I could teach about those
things, but I want to teach about something equally important.

Important

When I tell Ersu I want to teach all about soilnurture and looganuts, she nods her approval. *You are your father's daughter.* I swallow. I think this might be my opportunity to ask her about Papa, about what was wrong with him to make her go and never come back, but words stick in my throat. Didn't you love him? I want to ask. And as important: Didn't you love *me*?

I hide my face into D-39's neck because I am not ready to hear Ersu's answers. So I ask her about Zion instead. *How did she get here?* Ersu's eyes stare out at the distant humpbacks. *Her parents both died of BrkX. One of the dogs we brought over was infected, and it got loose and found their cabin, about six miles from here.* Ersu's voice is soft, so soft. I hardly breathe because I don't want to miss a word. *It was my fault.* She shakes her head. *I didn't catch it. Zion was left with no one. So I brought her home with me.* Her bright eyes meet mine. *You would have done the same.*

The Same

I see Zion differently after I know her story.
I make myself quirkface at her in the morn-
ings, and I say thank you when she hands
me a plate. Now whenever those jayballs
feelings wash over me, I remind myself that
Zion hasn't stolen anything from me. She's
a victim of BrkX, the deathstretch—like
me. Our stories may have different details,
but in so many ways, we're the same. And
most of the time it helps.

Warmer weather also helps. As soon as the
roads clear, we get a visitor at Everlake. I
squintcheck as she steers and parks her
truck. It isn't until she takes off her hat
and steps down that I recognize her half-
farmer, half-scientist coveralls. *Gloria*, she
says as she sweeps the hat down. *At your
service.*

It *is* Gloria! Gloria from the pit. *But—
How—* As she unloads things we can't
grow, like chocolate nubs and softcloth
paintbrushes, I can't get my words to come
out right. I knew Gloria had contact with
all kinds of people. Of course she knew
about Everlake. It just never occurred to

me to link the two. My thoughts whip-whirl. Maybe she knows other things, too. Like about what happened to Papa. I grab her hand. *Have you seen my father? Please tell me.*

Tell Me

Sorry, she says, in her matter-of-fact way. *Not since that day you two came to the pit.* My heart floods out. She hasn't seen Papa. Will I ever find out what happened? D-39 bumps her head against my leg.

D-39. Gloria was the one who said my robo was special. It was her words that convinced Papa to let me keep her. As I watch her hand Ersu a small green envelope, I get it. *You knew.* I step closer to her. *You knew D-39 was real.* She shakes her head. *I suspected. But I was thrown off by the Dog Alive logo and all the modifications.* All the air leaves my lungs. *But—* If she thought D-39 was real, she should have said something. *Why didn't you tell me or Papa?* Gloria doesn't stop unloading. *I wasn't sure at first. And then the robopatrol barged in. There wasn't time.* My mind scrambles back to that day at the pit, how fast Papa and I got out of there. How joyslammed I was, because it meant I was keeping D-39. And then the boomblast. Gloria couldn't have told us, even if she wanted to.

I meet her eyes. It all happened exactly the way it needed to. *So you're part of the K-9 Corridor.* Gloria quirkfaces. *Since the start.*

I stand there zapjawed until Ersu thrusts a little green envelope into my hands. *Here.* She quirkfaces. *This is for you, Klynt.* I lift my eyebrows. The envelope is so light I don't have any idea what it could be. Then I flip it over and see the picture printed on the front. *Looganut seeds?* She nods. *Don't know if they'll grow here, but we can try.*

We. *Yes.* I quirkface. *We can try.* Sometimes trying is the only thing to do.

Only Thing to Do

When Gloria grabs Ersu's hands, we all look at her. Her eyes are bright. *I wanted to say this straightaway, but I got sidetracked.* She offers me a small quirk, and I return it. Because we all know she was sidetracked by me. *The deathstretch,* she says. *It's over!*

My chest clutchjaws. *The deathstretch is over?* Gloria nods. *The Patriots infiltrated the capital last Thursday. With intel help from some of Vex's cabinet, the president was arrested!* Ersu and everyone start jumping and shouting and asking a jumble of questions.

Vex and his cronies are going to be tried for crimes against humanity, Gloria continues. *Meanwhile it's chaos in the Worselands. All taxes have been reverted. Property ownership will be reinstated, weapons will be returned. It will take some time to sort everything out, but it's going to happen.*

I can't believe it. The deathstretch is over. It's really over. *Papa,* I breathe. My steady, dependable Papa. What if real heroes are the ones who stay? The ones who stick it out and stay true to what they believe in and all they hold dear? I close my eyes. Papa never doubted that our side would win. *Elections for a new president are next month*, Gloria says.

I'm joyslammed about the news, but the only thing I can do is stand still. Because I don't really know yet what the end of the deathstretch means. I don't know yet if Papa is dead or living.

Living

Greenseason begins oh-so-slowly, but after a few weeks of steady sun and warmer temperatures, the Wilds are transformed. Not only do the looganuts grow, they flourish. With D-39 and Jopa by my side, I do all the things I once hated: digging, hoeing, bending, sweating. For everything I know how to do, I have a new question I wish I could ask Papa, who knows everything about looganut farming. *I like it here*, Jopa says, out of nowhere. *Don't you?* I pull off my gloves, give him my full attention. *Sure*, I say. *Why do you ask?* He shrugs. *You just seem different, that's all.*

I nudge him with my shoulder. I don't have to ask what he means, because I am different. I know I am. *Ersu's trying. So am I.* All those itchtwitchy parts—my hurt and my flipfury at Ersu—are being rubbed away. *Besides, just look at D-39.* Her belly is full again and her coat gleams. She's never been healthier or happier.

Each day the three of us work together in the fields, talking and snickergiggling.

No one is prouder than I am when the looganut stalks thicken and turn green-oh-so-green, their tight buds following the sun from morning until evening.

Evening

Jopa and I sit by the lake as the sun drops, painting the sky in purple and peach stripes. We take turns throwing a stick for D-39, who paddles after it again and again. Then she smells or hears something and comes back to shore empty-mouthed, ears cocked. She shakes the water out of her fur, then paces, whines. Like she did all those days in the burrow. *What is it, girl? Why is she acting like she's on high alert?*

When I look behind me, I know why.

Why

Two figures emerge from the woods. One a woman, hair pulled back in a ponytail. The other, chin up, steps quick, chewing on a pipe. Around his neck, a red bandana.

My heart catapults as I lift myself from the bank. *Papa?* Jopa leaps up. *Tiev?*

Tiev

I'm so zapjawed, I can't move. Papa hangs back as Tiev runs to Jopa and scoops her brother up. I get it right away—those invisible threads between me and Papa prickletwitch like they always have. He wants to give Tiev and Jopa their moment. So I follow his lead.

Mother didn't make it, Tiev says without preamble. *A rebel group boomblasted the clinic.* She clears her throat. *I couldn't tell you in the burrow—I didn't know how. That's why I used the sleeping drug.* She shakes her head, her ponytail brushing against her shoulders. *I was too puddleglum to deal with my own feelings, much less yours.*

She squeezes Jopa. *I didn't know what else to do. I needed time to deal with her death. So I went to rations day to stock up. I was going to wake you up when I got back. And then—* She doesn't have to say the rest. Not yet. *Please, Jopa.* She holds his face in her hands. *Say you forgive me.*

Jopa's eyes meet mine for the briefest moment before he focuses again on Tiev. He grabs her hands and holds them. *I forgive you.* He quirkfaces through his tears. *You're here. You're really here!* Finally Papa quirkfaces, too, and rushes toward me. *Oh, sugar girl,* he breathes. That's when I throw myself into his open arms.

Open Arms

D-39 prancedances around us as I squeeze Papa so hard it squashes all the air from my lungs. *Klynt!* The pipe clatters to the ground, and I can feel his cheek wet against mine. *Thank God.* Tears prick my eyes and suddenly I'm flipfurious, so flip-furious. I pummel his chest. *Why didn't you come back? We waited as long as we could!* His body is as solid as the trunk of an ancient leafgiant, and he stands there letting me pound on him. *I was so startle-spooked*, I tell him. *I didn't know what to do.* He grabs my shoulders. *I'm sorry, sugar girl. So, so sorry.* He lifts my chin, forcing me to meet his eyes. *I wanted so much to get back to you. But I couldn't get around all the blockades.*

Blockades

Papa holds me to his chest. His heart rammerjammers, just like mine. He tells me how government soldiers ignored the ceasefire and created blockades with lines of robofighters. *They didn't let anyone get their rations. People were starving and desperate—far worse off than us.* When he and others infiltrated the line and tried to sneak out rations to distribute, robosoldiers openfired. *We were trying to help,* Papa says. *Trying to make things right.*

He tells me that the people who avoided capture hid out in what used to be the school gym. *My school?* He nods. *That's where I found Tiev. The robosoldiers—* He chokes up for a minute. *They killed so many that day. We were lucky to find each other alive.* It takes a jinglesnap for all this to settle in. *So you didn't meet the lion-man? The one in Jopa's burrow?* Papa sighs. *Not alive.* He strokes my hair. *We were in hiding until the president was arrested and the robos were nulled.*

First thing Tiev and I did when the sirens rang out the all clear was go to the burrow.

We weren't half a mile away when we heard gunfire. People were scared, looting— He shakes his head, tells me how he, too, went jayballs, thinking Jopa and I were inside. *I ran like a wild gobbler, but there was no one left. The hatch was thrown, the place plundered. No one left alive.* He smooths my hair and lipbrushes the top of my head. *It was a close call.*

Close Call

I clamp my hands over my ears. I don't want to hear any more. Papa understands without me telling him. *You did the right thing, sugar girl. You had to leave. And you came here, where you knew I would find you!* I interrupt him. *But the map. D-39—* I blame myself for more than one close call. He holds a finger to my lips. *But nothing. I'm so proud of you, Klynt. You did what had to be done.*

What Had to Be Done

D-39 circles us, her tongue lolling and tail swishswiping. She's rounding us up, as if it's what must be done. My heart is beating double time when I realize Papa doesn't know about D-39 being real. *Papa—* I kneel and wrap my arm around my dog. *Wait until I tell you about D-39.* I can't stop the quirk from lifting my cheeks.

Papa squintchecks. *Tell me what?* When Papa scratches D-39 behind her ears, Jopa bounces over to us. *Tell him, K-K! Tell him right now.* Papa puts a hand on his hip. *Tell me what?* A snickergiggle burbles out of my throat. A real snickergiggle. *You're not going to believe it.*

Believe It

Try me, he says. Jopa circles us, his hands over his mouth, barely keeping the secret in. So I let it all come out in one big breath. *This is D-39, Papa! D-39 is real. She's a real dog!* His eyes go bigsky, and my heart fatrattles like jayballs. And then the words are streaming out of my mouth. How D-39 was disguised as a robo, part of the K-9 Corridor. How we found out and how we got here to Everlake. And how Gloria knew.

Papa shakes his head, slowing me down, stopping me. *I can't believe it. A real dog. Wow.* He rubs D-39's belly and lets her lick his fingers. *If that doesn't beat it all.* While Jopa introduces Tiev to his new ants, Papa shows me scars: slices on his back, knife wound in his ribs, gunshot through his thigh from the day of the blockade. *But I'm here now, thanks to the Patriots banding together. Not giving up.*

The deathstretch is over, Klynt. Me, you, D-39—we're the lucky ones. We all get a new beginning.

Beginning

The next night I shadow Ersu through her checkups of a few of the dogs. When the last dog has been loved, she sends Zion on an errand and turns to me. *Shall we visit the endstops?*

I nod because I like the endstops now, even if they are for dogs, not people. A quiet resting place for Ruby and all the others I never knew. Ersu and I can have a private conversation there.

We walk in silence, but when we pass the gate, Ersu sits on the ground in front of one of the markers. *It wasn't easy*, she starts. I wait, because I don't know exactly what she's talking about. *But I knew you were in good hands.*

Good Hands

I knew your father would take the best care of you. She looks up. *You didn't need me, see? And all these dogs*—she sweeps her arm through the air—*without me, they wouldn't have lived the lives they were meant to.* She grabs my hand, and it sends a thunderjolt up my arm and into my chest.

My mother's hands, so warm and strong—good hands. *You understand, don't you?* I don't. Not really. And I don't want to. Not when Papa is here.

I want you to know, she says. *You can stay here, all of you. You, Jopa, Tiev, D-39, your father. You don't have to go back to the Worselands if you don't want to.* I don't know what to say. Everlake has been a good place to be, but it's not my home. Still, I don't want to ruin this moment. I squeeze Ersu's hand, and she squeezes back. And when a blusterblow tickles the leafgiants, it sounds like *yessssss.*

Yessssss

Everyone at Everlake treats Papa and
Tiev like they've always been part of the
community. Zion's shy about interacting
with Papa, which surprises me a little.
Then I remember what happened to her
father. *Papa*, I say the next morning after
breakfast. *I want you to know that Zion is
someone very important.* I swallow, and
make my voice come out strong. *Zion is my
sister.* Because in the ways that matter,
yes, she is. She upcuddles me then, her
braid swinging into my face, smelling of
rosemary. It makes me wish I'd said those
words much sooner.

When I show Papa the looganuts, his eyes
fill with tears. *They're beautiful*, he says,
and I tell him about Nuni and Dr. Wesl, the
border and the refugee camp. His favorite
part is about me and Jopa pulling D-39.
And the bowline didn't slip? I shake my
head and lean into his hand, the way D-39
always leans into mine. Yet another way to
show love.

Love

Papa lifts my chin so his eyes meet mine. *Ersu says we should breed D-39. Let her have a litter of puppies. Would you like that?*

I gasp. Would I like that? *Papa, I would love that!* He continues. *And if you want to stay here at Everlake*—he takes a breath—*with your mother, you can do that. She says you are welcome to stay.* I scan his face with all its lines and creases. *What about you?* I say. *Do you want to stay?*

He shakes his head. *No. I can't live here. I belong at the Anchor T. It's where I've always belonged.* I can't help it: I quirkface. Because for once Papa and I are on exactly the same page. No matter how peaceful Everlake has been, it's not what I want.

I want to go home. With you. To the Anchor T. I lean my head against his shoulder. *Ersu's not*— I swallow. It's hard to find the right words. *She's my mother, but not really.* His eyes meet mine, wet with understanding. *You really want to rebuild the farm?* I nod. I am a restoration expert, after all. *We should get started as soon as possible.*

As Soon as Possible

Two weeks later we set out—me, Papa, Jopa and Tiev, and a hopefully pregnant D-39—to cross the border back into the Worselands.

I invite Zion to visit us sometime soon, and her freckle-stars shine. *It won't be the same without you here,* she says. That's true. I am not the same either. Nothing will ever be the same. *I'll never forget you, I promise.* She quirkfaces. *Thank you.*

When I upcuddle Ersu goodbye, she thrusts a pair of hand-knit gloves into my hands. *For next freezeseason.* I quirkface. We both know they're not really for me—they're for D-39 to steal.

As we walk away from Everlake, I hear a voice. *Yes. Go home.* Not Mama's voice. Not Papa's or anyone else's.

Mine.

Mine

I stop in the middle of the trail. What if being a hero isn't about staying or going, or even about fighting or rescuing. What if being a hero is about listening? To yourself?

Yes, I think, as one hand sinks into the warmth of D-39's back. That's it, isn't it? A hero listens to her own voice above all others. The way I've listened to mine.

My fingers find the old rainbow sky-sail, and I pull it out of my pack. I hold it steady while Jopa runs ahead until a blusterblow catches the tattered fabric and sends it soaring high over the leafgiants.

For the first time in a while, I think of my old printing press. I can't wait to rebuild my museum. I grab Papa's hand in mine. *Let's go home.*

Home

After hours, days, weeks, it's all blue skies and quirkfacing over the looganuts. We spend part of every day sparkshining the land, rebuilding.

It takes a long while, but eventually I find all the parts I need to get the ham back up and running. I can't wait to broadcast, to tell Mama and Zion that D-39 had seven puppies. Seven! Soon I'll show the pups the fields and the pond and the burrow.

When school starts back next month, Papa says we'll bring the pups so they can find new homes—except the black one. That one belongs to Jopa. His name is Ant. And maybe—if I can convince him—Papa will let me keep one, too.

I stroke the grunting pile of puppies and hardpress my face into D-39's neckfur. *Thank you*, I say. Which is also what I want to say to the world, in spite of—and because of—everything.

I click the button. *Hey hi ho there . . .*

GLOSSARY

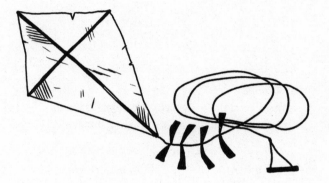

bigsky: wide, or to widen
blusterblow: wind
boomblasts: bombs
burrow: underground shelter
bzzflopped: electronically broken or dead
chug-chug: tractor
chugspew: vomit
cockadoodle: rooster
cold-dust: snow
cressnut: an edible nut
deathstretch: war
dirtdust: a mix of soil, grit, and grime
downcount: make a final countdown
dripface: cry
droopbottom: sad
endstop: gravestone
fatrattle: make a clatter or loud sound
firstgen: first generation (first of something)
fistclench: tighten
flipfurious: angry
flutterbugged: nervous
flutterbugs: butterflies
freezeseason: winter
freshwash: rain
fussfidget: repair or adjust in an
    experimental way
glimmerspark: shine
gobbler: turkey
go jayballs: get upset or excited
greenseason: spring
halfdug: a home built into the side of a hill
hardpress: apply firm pressure
hardwipe: reset or erase all previous data
hotseason: summer

humdrummed: bored
hum-nothing: isolated, lonely
humpbacks: mountains
humpgrump: grumpy
itchglitchy: prone to malfunction
itchtwitchy: trembly
jagsaw: go from straight to crooked
jayballs: ridiculous
jinglesnap: short moment
joyslammed: happy
knockaround: leisure, spare or free, as in time
leafgiant: tree
leafseason: autumn
lipbrush: kiss
looganuts: a soybean/canola hybrid crop
    harvested for meal and oil
meatscramble: canned meat product
m-fuel: a futuristic biofuel (short for
    miracle fuel)
must-dos: chores
needlebender: an artist who knits, crochets,
    or weaves fiber products
nulled: deactivated/canceled
panchobean: a variation of pinto bean
poopflush: toilet
prickletwitch: pucker or get a sudden feeling of
    excitement as felt through one's skin
puddleglum: sad
quirk: a smile
quirkface: to smile
quiverquake: lightly shake
ramjammed: stuck in place, difficult to dislodge
rammerjammer: quick, light beat or vibration
ramscramble: rush

rawfire: red and inflamed

ripclaw: tear away

robo: slang for robot

robofighter: a robotic plane or person used in war

scratchpatched: scuffed, chipped, or roughened
by wear

shuddershake: heave or move in a big, violent way

shutterbug: blink

skysail: kite

slipslop: someone/something who slobbers

slipsloppy: messy, often in a moist way

snickergiggle: laugh

soilnurture: gardening

sparkshine: clean/polish

squintcheck: squint

startlespooked: scared

streamscreen: TV or computer monitor

sweetmurmur: whisper

sweetsavage: wild, but not threatening

swishswipe: move back and forth in a constant,
gentle motion

thudjam: steady, repetitive knocking sound

ticktock: clock

tidywipe: wipe down or clean

upcuddle: hug

washdown: bath

waterworld: ocean

wheatkins: bread and crackers made from wheat

whifflegust: breathe heavily

whiprattle: make a rapidly repeating sound

whipwhirl: spin quickly and with urgency

whirlswirl: spin gently

zapjawed: surprised/shocked

zapper: a stinging insect

Author's Note

A few years ago I happened upon an online conversation among poets in which the question was posed: "Why are there no dystopian verse novels?" Could it be done? Would it work? *Yes*, I thought. Yes, yes, yes. And so I started working on what I then called my "boy-dog-war" story. Over the years I kept tinkering (as Klynt would!), and the story morphed into the girl-robodog-deathstretch book you hold in your hands.

The deathstretch was heavily influenced by the history of the Syrian Civil War. My inspiration for the Worselands was the beautiful state of North Dakota, which I've visited many times, thanks to my father, Ken Dykes Sr., who lived in Bismarck for nearly a decade. Papa and I both fell in love with the state's history, geography, and people. The D-39-model robodog was inspired by current quadruped robots powered by methanol (and how emerging technology will improve these machines). Klynt's Museum of Fond Memories is in honor of Jim Reed Books and the Museum of Fond Memories located in downtown Birmingham, Alabama.

I chose to present this story in prose poems because each poem acts as a burrow, offering readers a safe place to experience invented words and a dystopian reality. The technique of using the last words of one poem to serve as the title of the next poem is a variation on a traditional "crown" of sonnets—because in Klynt's world, the old is often bumping up against the new.

Writing this book allowed me to explore big ideas about freedom and heroism, as well as more intimate ones about love—like how complicated relationships can be between a child and a parent, and how impactful the bonds are between a child and a pet. I'm grateful to Rebecca Davis for first encouraging this idea and to Karen Boss for embracing Klynt and D-39 so completely and helping me grow this story and deliver it to the world. Thanks also to my entire family, and especially to Paul, who makes up the best words; to Andrew, who always champions all my stories; to Eric, who is passionate about freedom; to Mama and Papa, whose voices I hear every day; and to Sasha, Ruby, and Rosie—best dogs ever. 🐾